For my Dad, who always did the voices when he read me stories. Love you xxx

MISCHIEF MOST FORTUITOUS

Malignant House was uncharacteristically full. There were just two days left until the annual All Hallows' Haunt and it would be a race against time to get everything ready.

The All Hallows' Haunt – AHH! for short – was a ball, but a ball like no other. It took place each year on Halloween. The AHH! was a chance for the Underlanders and Topunders to get dressed up in their finery and have a good old party. It was also a

time for dodgy deals to be struck and old feuds to be buried, with fresh ones dug up in their place. The All Hallows' Haunt was the most anticipated event in any Topunder's calendar. And this year, finally, Ma and Pa would be hosting it.

Underland is the land of the dead where ghosts, witches, ghouls, vampires and all those of a deceased variety live; they are called Underlanders.

Topside is the ordinary world. But Topunders are far from ordinary. Topunders like to walk on the shadier side of life. They are able to converse with the dead and undead, and travel freely between Underland and Topside. Many Topunders live Topside because that's where they can make the most money through swindles, trickery and good honest heists. And because the gullible Topsiders are always ripe for a mischievous pranking.

The art of mischief is taken very seriously by Topunders. The Maligns were mischief-makers by

trade; it was a proud profession passed down through the generations since Maximus Maligmus had come over during the Roman conquest of AD 43.

But Malice, like her grandad and her uncle Vex, preferred a merrier kind of mischief-making to her parents. She also liked bathing, reading and not keeping earwigs behind her ears. These things had conspired to cause tensions between her and her parents in the past, so they were all working on their understanding and embracing of each other's differences, even though it wasn't always easy.

The Malign family consisted of Ma, Pa, Grandad, Malice, Antipathy-Rose and Uncle Vex. They lived in Malignant House, the Malign ancestral home – apart from Uncle Vex, who

lived and worked down in Underland. Malignant House was a teetering gothic mansion brooding in the corner of Felicity Square, where it was considered to be a boil on the bum of the terribly fancy neighbourhood.

Every year the Topunder family who made the most mischief was given the honour of hosting the All Hallows' Haunt. The Malign family had missed out on this privilege for the last century, largely due to one or two Maligns whose rejection of malicious mischief had brought down the family's mischief average.

For the past few years, the ball had been hosted in turns by the Edinburgh MacNe'erdoowell family and the Gravesend Grudges. When Malice had joined her Uncle Vex – a private Underland investigator and infamous do-gooder – as an apprentice detective, the Malign family's mischief average had dropped

even further. There had seemed little hope that the glory of hosting would ever come their way, despite her parents' tireless mischief efforts.

However, this year an event of mischief most fortuitous had befallen the Maligns. Grandad had won the coordinates to some buried treasure in a game of poker. He gave the coordinates to Pa, who found the treasure chest buried in Samphire Hoe near Dover.

Inside the chest, as well as the usual gold goblets, doubloons and strings of pearls, were two cutlass swords, their hilts studded with gems the size of golf balls. Ma took the cutlass swords into an antique jewellers to have them appraised.

Unfortunately – or fortunately in Ma's case – when Ma entered the jewellers, wearing her usual sour expression and brandishing two gleaming swords, the staff assumed it was a heist and hastily stuffed all the shops antiques into a large sack and handed it over to Ma. Ma still doesn't know what the cutlass swords are worth, but she did come away with eighty-two and a half thousand pounds worth of loot, so she didn't feel inclined to complain.

When the All Hallows' Haunt Association – AHHA! for short – heard about the Maligns' marvellously monstrous mischief-making, they immediately awarded them the task of hosting this year's All Hallows' Haunt. It was the single most important thing to have ever happened to the Malign family. Preparations were in full swing; the Maligns were going all out to make this the best All Hallows' Haunt ever!

PIXIES WERE PESKY
AT BEST!

In the old formal kitchens below stairs, not used
by the family, two head chefs – one alive and
one dead – were preparing fiendishly disgusting
canapés ahead of the festivities. Delicacies such
as frogs' eye blinis and tempura
toenails would sit beside
more traditional nibbles
like satay slugs and
earwax dip.

Not all Topunder tastebuds were quite so sophisticated and so there would be toffee-apple pies and popcorn pavlovas for those who preferred simpler fare. A croquembouche as tall as Uncle Vex was being constructed. Each little bun was filled with vanilla pumpkin cream and the tower was held together with candied spider silk. Ghosts in chefs' whites and mop-capped scullery maids flitted about the ancient kitchen absorbed in their tasks. Malice and her sister had already been shooed out of the kitchen once that morning for stealing ghoulberry meringues.

Above stairs, the ballroom had been transformed. For many decades it had been used as a dumping ground for the excess swag and treasure acquired dishonestly by the Malign family. But with the All Hallows' Haunt approaching, Ma and Pa had shifted and shovelled the loot out of the ballroom and arranged it in artful mounds all around

the house so that their ill-gotten gains could be admired by all.

The heap in the entrance hall displayed spoils collected during Ma and Pa's deep-sea dives to shipwrecks. Sitting proudly on top of the doubloons and silver tankards was a ship's figurehead made of solid gold (possibly one of the reasons why the ship sank). The figurehead was a Viking with a long golden beard, a horned helmet and two Ceylon sapphires for eyes. Legend had it that if you spat in the Viking's left eye it would grant you a wish, but it had never worked yet … and Malice had *really* tried.

The dining room displayed the royal mounds: rings, watches, necklaces and all manner of swag swiped from members of the royal families down the centuries. Mary, Queen of Scots' favourite cameo necklace hung from King Ethelred the Unready's sword, which nestled beside a small gold brooch

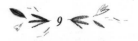

with a painting of two corgis in the middle. Ma had pinched the corgi brooch from Queen Elizabeth's lapel when her majesty was on a walkabout in Hull. It was one of Ma's proudest achievements.

Malice bypassed the ghosts fixing up a guillotine for the party photobooth and ducked beneath a garland of broken glass and deadly nightshade to enter the ballroom.

She had never seen the ballroom empty before. It was vast. Secrets hidden by the swag for hundreds of years were now revealed. Magical mirrors ran the length of two walls. The glass was speckled with the patina of age as it replayed smoky images of long-dead guests dancing waltzes in crinoline gowns and white powdered wigs from All Hallows' Haunts gone by. The floor beneath Malice's feet was a dusty chequerboard of cold marble. *How many feet have danced on these tiles?* she wondered.

"Malice!" came her ma's hellcat screech. "Come 'ere, I need your advice on which tiara to wear."

Malice left the ballroom and hurried upstairs, narrowly missing a spectre on a ladder applying extra fungus to the walls above the grand staircase.

The house was being decorated all over to embrace Halloween and the All Hallows' Haunt. Jack-o'-lanterns grinned out from every surface and papier mâché witches on broomsticks flew through the air, courtesy of a spell by Nana Rascally. Grandad played poker with a banshee (a lovely spirit with a terrible reputation) who had agreed to wail and moan through the water pipes to infuse the house with a spooky ambience. To be fair, Malignant House was already pretty spooky, what with skeletons in almost every cupboard and ghosts floating around all day and night. But Ma and Pa really wanted to push the

boat out for the All Hallows' Haunt. So, the walls were hung with black bunting and pumpkin fairy lights and Ma had ordered in eight hundred extra house spiders to ensure there were an abundance of cobwebs hanging from the ceilings and light fittings.

Malice had invited the bats, who lived in the attic rooms, downstairs to flit around the house and add an extra layer of eerie. Some Topunder's were born with special gifts. Malice had witch ancestry and her special gift was that she could talk with creatures of the night. She had a special affinity with moths, but she also enjoyed conversations with bats, owls, foxes, badgers and even wolves on occasion.

Pa had caught several pixies from the gardens and let them loose in the house to play tricks on guests. He thought this was a hilariously mischievous idea. Malice begged to differ. Pixies were pesky at best; they had already deconstructed all her socks into

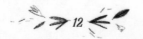

balls of wool and eaten her science project.

"Malice Morbid Malign!" Ma screeched again and the bats – who have very sensitive ears – dived into an umbrella stand for cover.

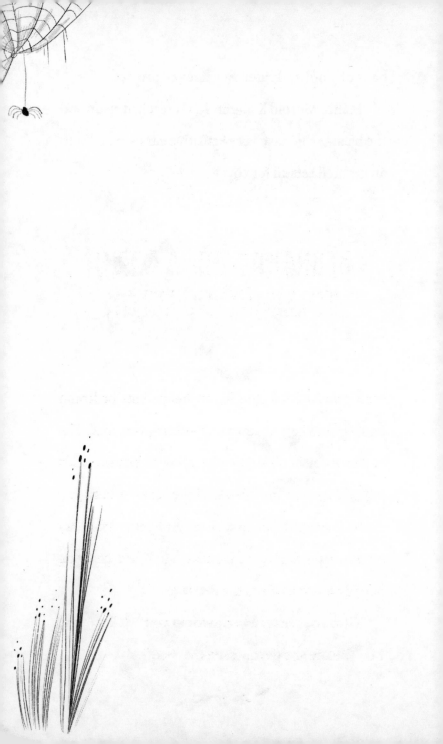

BERNARD WAS A VERY TOLERANT SKELETON

Malice pushed open the door to her parents' bedroom and plonked herself down on the four-poster bed. The bed groaned and listed to the left with a downwards jolt. Malice bent and lifted the frilly valance sheet. Just as she suspected; her baby sister, Antipathy-Rose, lay on the carpet amongst the balls of sock fluff, gnawing happily away at one of the bed legs.

"Give your sister a bone would you, Malice," said Ma. "Before she devours *another* bed."

Antipathy-Rose had exceedingly strong sharp teeth. Pa had great plans to take her safe-cracking with him when she was a bit older.

Malice crossed the room and pulled open a cupboard door. Bernard the skeleton was hiding in there. Antipathy-Rose had burned her bridges with him after she'd had a good nibble on his shin bone last week. Bernard was a very tolerant skeleton, but he had his limits, and having his limbs nibbled was one of them. Bernard pressed a bony finger to his mouth in the universal code for 'Shhhh'.

"Don't worry, Bernard," Malice whispered. "I've got you covered."

She reached above his head and pulled a box of cow bones down from the shelf.

"I asked the butcher if I could take his beef bones off his hands. Told him I had a large dog!" She winked at Bernard, who's jaw jiggled, and he held his ribs to stop them clacking as he chuckled. Malice closed the cupboard door and handed a long shin bone to Antipathy-Rose, who immediately ceased whittling the bed leg and turned her attention to the new treat.

"Go easy," said Malice. "There are no more bones till teatime."

Antipathy-Rose smiled creepily and licked her lips.

Malice sat back down on the sloping bed. Ma's dressing table was laden with tiaras. There must have been about thirty, all pinched and pilfered down the centuries by various members of the Malign family. The jewel-encrusted headdresses twinkled in the light of the gas lamps which dimly lit her parents' cobweb-strewn bedroom.

"Now," said Ma, nestling each tiara in turn into her snake like coils of hair. "Which one is best? Which one says magisterial mischief-maker?"

Malice cocked her head to one side as Ma switched between tiaras.

"I think I like the one that has all the diamond skulls with rubies for eyes," Malice mused.

Ma sniffed.

"You could be right. More than the one with the hissing gargoyles?"

"That's more of an everyday tiara, I think."

"Skulls it is then," said Ma. "I want that Mordacious MacNe'erdoowell to be green with envy when she sees me in my finery. I'm gonna make her rue the day she called me a mediocre mischief-maker!"

The MacNe'erdoowells and the Maligns had enjoyed an unhealthy rivalry since the time of the Domesday Book. They contrived to be just barely civil on the surface, but beneath the stale air-kisses and clammy handshakes there simmered a loathing that could sour milk.

When the hosts were announced for this year's All Hallows' Haunt, Mordacious MacNe'erdoowell was so incensed that she and her life partner Truculent had sent a bouquet of fresh roses with their heads still attached – the ultimate in disgusting – and a card which read *May the sun shine upon your All Hallows' Haunt and all the flowers in your garden be in full bloom. And may*

your menace be minor, you mediocre mischief-maker, and your dreams be sweet with giggling cherubs. Kisses of death, Mordacious.

These were threatening words indeed.

"Will all the Topunder families be at the ball?" Malice asked.

"All the ones we've invited," said Ma slyly.

Malice rolled her eyes. To not invite a Topunder family to the All Hallows' Haunt was a huge insult, one that could have repercussions for years to come. Malice wondered why her parents made life so difficult for themselves. It was true that Topunder families were rarely what you'd call "friendly" with each other but since their lives were entwined anyway, Malice didn't see why they wouldn't at least want to keep things civil.

"So, who *have* you invited?"

Ma screwed her face up while she concentrated.

"The Welsh Maggots and the Stonehenge

Stenches. The Gravesend Grudges and the Edinburgh MacNe'erdoowells, obviously. Then there's the Yorkshire Tealeaves, the Midland Meddlers, the Devonshire Deviants and the Norwich Connivers."

Malice ran through the names of the families not mentioned by Ma in her head: the Pinchers, the Racketeers, the Brigands and the Savages hadn't been invited to the Haunt. Oh dear!

It was tit for tat really. Topunders never "turned the other cheek" or "let sleeping dogs lie". Oh no, for every slight upon them they paid it back double, no matter how long it took. Six years ago, the Shropshire Pinchers hadn't invited the Maligns to *their* All Hallows' Haunt. Ten years ago, Gaseous Racketeer had excluded Pa from a bank heist. In the winter of 1984 Phlegm Brigand had beaten Ma at Monopoly. Last year, the Savage family went on the trip of a lifetime to Transylvania and had been rubbing everyone's noses in it ever since. And now

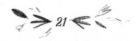

the time had come at last for Ma and Pa to take their revenge on all the little snubs and gripes that had been inflicted upon them down the decades. Malice sighed as she listened to Ma twitter on about all the mischief-makers who would be sick with jealousy over the Malign's recent successes.

A PARAGON OF
MISCHIEVOUSNESS

Malice finished helping Ma untangle a tiara of black scorpions from her hair and said, "I've got to go, Ma. Can you keep Antipathy-Rose out of my bedroom, please? Between her and the pixies, I'll have nothing left."

"Did you just say *please*?" Ma snapped. "I thought we taught you better than that, young lady."

"Sorry," said Malice, brushing her foot across the dusty carpet.

"I will not have good manners in this house. You're lucky Pa wasn't here. Where you off to anyway?"

"I'm meeting Seth in the mausoleum."

Seth was Malice's best friend, and he was also a Topsider: two things guaranteed to make you unpopular in any Topunder household.

Ma's lips thinned to straight lines, like two raspberry shoelaces stretched across her mouth. She didn't approve of Seth, or friends in general, but she couldn't deny that he had been useful to the Malign family on several occasions now, and that made him just about bearable.

Ma sniffed. "I wouldn't mind so much if he made an effort, but he's just so darned" – she covered her mouth as she heaved – "friendly!" she finished weakly. "It's unnerving."

"But he is allowed to the All Hallows' Haunt, isn't he? You did promise."

Ma huffed but nodded as she began to sift through a box of pilfered necklaces to find one that matched her tiara.

"Just keep him away from the baby. I don't want him being a good influence on her."

Antipathy-Rose peered round the side of the bed and grinned at Malice, her sharp little teeth glinting in the soft light. Malice's sister had taken a shine to Seth, but Malice wasn't yet sure whether Antipathy-Rose wanted him to be her friend or a chew-toy.

"Ooooheeeeee!" a sound like a seagull being strangled bounced off the walls. Malice winced at the unmistakable voice of Vendetta Grudge. Ma's

25

eyes lit up and she quickly flung on some extra jewels.

Ma and Pa didn't have friends; it wasn't the mischief-maker way. They had business associates and they had acquaintances. Animosity and Vendetta Grudge were acquaintances, and the closest approximation her parents would allow to friends.

Vendetta Grudge clip-clopped into Ma's bedroom in a pair of towering stilettos. She had the smallest feet and ankles Malice had ever seen on an adult. These ballooned up into enormously wide calves, enrobed in fishnet tights, so that they resembled two pink hams in a net.

Ma was, in her own way, quite glamorous, dripping as she permanently was in stolen jewellery and haute couture. But Vendetta was next level. Even in the middle of summer, she wore a yeti fur coat – the yeti had supposedly died of natural causes – which smelled like the bottom of a gerbil cage. Her bosoms protruded out from her coat like a shelf upon which

26

all manner of bejewelled necklaces were balanced. Many years of wearing frightfully heavy earrings meant that her earlobes rested on her shoulders like two diamond studded tote bags.

"Vendetta, darling!" Ma crooned as the two women exchanged air kisses, noses wrinkled in distaste. "You look as gaudy as ever."

"Tetchy-Sue!" Vendetta screeched. "You look positively gaunt! Now I know you're busy with the All Hallows' preparations – you not being so used to high society gatherings as what I am. So, I made you a casserole."

She proffered a glass oven dish in which something brown and sludgy blipped and puffed out powdery spores.

"It's a mildew mushroom bake. I picked the most poisonous mushrooms myself." She thrust the dish at Malice. "Put it somewhere warm and damp where it can fester."

Malice took the dish. An earthy, mouldering smell emanated up from the casserole and Malice's stomach growled; she was very into vegetarian cuisine at the moment.

"Vendetta, you shouldn't have," said Ma ungraciously.

"I know," Vendetta replied.

Malice turned to leave.

"See you later, Ma," Malice called.

"Where's she off to?" sniffed Vendetta.

Ma faltered.

"Oh, she's just going to, um, she has to, she likes to…"

"I'm going to deposit live toads on the doorsteps of all the houses in Felicity Square, then ring their doorbells and run away," said Malice quickly. She winked at Ma and Ma gave her a grateful smile. It wouldn't do for the Grudges to know that Malice didn't do mischief-making, or that she was fraternizing with a topsider in the mausoleum.

Vendetta looked impressively sour.

"You've got her well trained," she sneered. "Of course, my Maudlin's just been given a place at the Fagin School of Pickpocketing, so he doesn't have time for that kind of minor-mischief any more. He is *very* sneaky," she added proudly.

Maudlin was the Grudges' son, and he was a bit older than Malice. She had tried to make conversation with him once or twice at Topunder parties, but he preferred scowling and skulking to chatting.

Maudlin was held up as a paragon of mischievousness. Sometimes, when Vendetta boasted about Maudlin's achievements in roguery, Malice thought she could see wistfulness in Ma's expression – as though Ma wished Malice could be more like him.

It made Malice's heart ache. She didn't want to be a let-down to her parents, but she didn't want to let *herself* down either by trying to be something she wasn't. Families were tricky.

A TALENT FOR
THE STINKING ARTS

Malice left Ma and Vendetta to talk about the Haunt preparations and gossip about the other Topunder families who would be attending. Still carrying the stinky casserole dish, she clomped down the sweeping staircase of the crumbling family mansion.

Malice took the casserole to the kitchen where she found Animosity Grudge sitting in an armchair by the fire, chatting with Grandad. Grandad was Malice's most favourite ghost. He split his time between

the attic, where they did puzzles and homework together, and the Queenie Florus Grandads' Club down in Underland, where he played poker and drank stinging-nettle tea. He could see the good in everyone, even when they hid it really well.

By contrast, Animosity could only see in people what would be of benefit to him. He was a tall, thin man, who wore an oversized black leather jacket because he thought it made him look like a tough geezer, but it actually made him look like he was wearing someone else's clothes. He had long, greasy matted hair with a beard and personality to match. Pa thought he was a real cool dude. Malice thought he was sneaky. But you couldn't choose your parents' "friends" for them.

Animosity was dripping Ma's latest stink-bomb concoction on to his lanky grey beard and massaging it in.

"Greetings, maggot," he said jovially. His voice

was deep as thunder and scratchy as a rockfall, so that even when he was being friendly he sounded like he wanted to eat you alive. "Sterling stuff this," he continued, lifting his beard up to his nose and inhaling deeply. "Tetchy-Sue should branch into aftershaves."

"I keep telling her," said Grandad, "she's got a talent for the Stinking Arts. But you know what it's like, working mum and all that. She just hasn't got the time, what with running the Haunting Agency and keeping on top of the mischief-making."

Ma and Pa owned a haunting agency in Underland. They rented Topsider houses to Underland ghosts so that they could haunt the families who lived there. It was a lucrative business. There were plenty of troublesome spooks in the Haunting Quarter of Underland who would pay good money to move into a nice Topside house and scare the pants off the unsuspecting occupants.

Animosity nodded gravely. "Where in purgatory is Pugnacious?" he asked.

Malice placed the casserole dish down on the stove, where one of the kitchen ghosts eyed it with suspicion.

"He's still on his morning mischief rounds," answered Grandad.

Animosity gave a derisive tut.

"I make Maudlin do my morning mischief shifts. It's good training for when he takes over the family business – means I can concentrate on matters in Underland." Animosity smoothed some of Ma's stink-bomb juice through his hair. "Yes, siree," he

continued. "Our Maudlin is quite the menace. He's got ideas for mischief-making that will revolutionize the way we cause mayhem. Me and his ma are very proud of his troublesome nature."

Malice sighed inwardly. More praise for Maudlin's mischief. Grandad caught her eye and smiled knowingly.

"Our Malice has a few tricks of her own," he said. "She's going to make a real difference in the world."

Malice felt a warm glow in her chest and wondered if she was shining on the outside.

Animosity just frowned in confusion. "'Make a difference'? What kind of *difference*? Your pa should be making you do his mischief, you little pustule. I've heard you're a right mischief slacker!" he added.

"Pa likes to make his own mischief; he's very proud of his shenanigans," said Malice. "He takes it very seriously."

"Meh," Animosity snorted. "Hard work never did

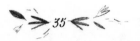

35

no one no good. Slovenly is the way forward. Next you'll be telling me he's started recycling!"

They all had a jolly good laugh at that.

Malice excused herself saying she had to steal the local children's pocket money, of which Animosity heartily approved.

PRACTISING THE MAGIC OF MOTH-WHISPERING

As Malice made her way through the gardens –
plucking a pixie from her pinafore and relocating
him in a dahlia flower – she bumped into Pa. He was
on his way back from his weekly mischief-making
trip to the supermarket.

"Hello, Pa, was there satisfactory mischief today?"
Malice asked.

"Not too shabby," Pa replied, grinning smugly. "I
superglued all the trolleys together in the car park,

let off one of Ma's stink bombs in the vegetable aisle and swapped over all the front covers of the dailies on the news stand so that everyone buys the wrong newspaper."

Malice raised her eyebrows.

"Well," said Malice. "I'm off to the mausoleum. The Grudges are at the house. Animosity is waiting for you in the kitchen."

Pa grinned and rubbed his hands together with glee.

"I've been waiting for him to come over so I could show him this!" Pa lifted up his sleeve to show a clear retractable tube about the width of a drinking straw strapped to his wrist, which disappeared up his shirt sleeve. He then pointed to his collar and Malice could see that the tube must run all the way up his arm because it poked out of the neck of his shirt.

"What is it?" Malice asked.

"It's a jammy doughnut jam-stealing device," he said. "When I'm at the cake counter of the

supermarket, I release the tube, like so." Pa bent his wrist back and the tube slipped forward. He produced a sugary doughnut covered in fluff from his trouser pocket. "Then I casually spear a doughnut on the counter," he demonstrated this by poking the tube into the doughnut. "Then I suck out all the jam!" He trained his mouth down to the top of the tube sticking out of his collar and began to suck. "I can surreptitiously slurp the jam out of a dozen doughnuts in under a minute," he said proudly.

"Works on custard doughnuts too. And when I'm done, I simply retract the tube and go on my way, with none of those silly Topsiders any the wiser."

He grinned.

"That is pure mischief, Pa," said Malice. She couldn't deny she was impressed.

"That means a lot to me," said Pa, tearing up.

"Animosity will be well impressed," said Malice. "I've got to go, Seth's waiting for me for moth practice."

"Righty-ho." Pa was jovial – he wasn't keen on Seth's do-gooder habits, but he did appreciate them practising the magic of moth-whispering. It was important to keep the old traditions alive and, in Pa's view, it couldn't hurt to have a moth-whisperer in the family.

Malice found Seth sitting outside the mausoleum, a little cloud of moths above his head. The mausoleum was a stone building with columns and

fearsome gargoyles leering out from every corner. It was where the tombs of the Malign family ancestors were held, not that any of them stayed in their tombs! From the outside, the building didn't look much bigger than a beach hut – a grisly, haunted kind of beach hut – but inside, stairs led down to different levels and catacombs far below the surface. In the 1920s an archaeologist attempted to chart the labyrinth of tunnels below the mausoleum; as far as anyone knows, he's still down there.

"You didn't have to wait for me out here," said Malice, smiling. She was always pleased to see her best friend. Seth was the calm to her worry and Malice was the caution to his reckless; they made a good team.

Seth plucked a moth out of his ear; moths are inquisitive creatures.

"I'm not so keen on being in the mausoleum by myself. The ghosts like to practise their latest

haunting techniques on me."

"Ahh, I see." Malice nodded. "It's important for them to keep their skills up. Even ghosts have to move with the times."

Seth eyed her curiously. "I hadn't thought of it like that."

Though Seth was a Topsider, he was far from ordinary. He wasn't fazed by the strangeness of Malice's family life; if anything, he relished it. They had gravitated towards one another at school – two misfits adrift in a sea of ordinary – and had been best friends ever since. In a strange coincidence, one of Seth's dads, Bill, had been at university with Uncle Vex. Or maybe it wasn't a coincidence; maybe Seth and Malice had been destined to become friends – once you accepted that ghosts, vampires and the kraken were real, believing in destiny didn't seem like such a leap.

A MARVELLOUS KERFUFFLE

Malice and Seth settled themselves on two big cushions between the stone tombs of Hellion Malign and Frenzied-Mai Malign and began moth-whispering practice. Each week, Grandad set them a training worksheet to follow. The art of communing with moths took patience, which was why Ma and Pa couldn't do it. You had to be a good listener because moth voices are as soft a sound as their beating wings. Moth-whispering had helped Malice out of any number of scrapes; Moths could carry

SOS messages or nibble through ropes or swarm to create a diversion. It really was a very handy skill for a trainee investigator to have. Plus, moths were very interesting creatures once you got to know them.

They had just begun the third task on the worksheet – to learn the moth-whisperers' code of conduct – when an ear-piercing scream sent loitering ghosts diving for cover and caused Seth to jump into Malice's lap.

EEEK ARRGHH EEEK ARRGHH EEEK ARRGHH...

"What is that?" Seth shouted.

The shrieking siren was blasting up out of the catacombs below them.

"It's the Underland high alert!" Malice called back, motioning for Seth to abandon the mausoleum.

They pushed the door shut behind them, but the siren could still be heard.

"Come on!" Malice called, grabbing Seth's hand and pulling him towards Malignant House.

They reached the house and burst in through the kitchen, where Pa was busy tuning an old wireless to BBC Radio Ghoul FM.

Animosity was salivating with excitement and his wife's heaving bosoms caused her jewels to ripple like waves across her chest.

Ma, who was holding Antipathy-Rose in her arms, sniffed when she saw Seth and held her nose.

"PeeEww!" she exclaimed. "It stinks of soap and cleanliness round here!"

"Hello, Mrs Malign, it's fearsome to meet you again. I must say you're looking pinched," said Seth in his usual friendly tone.

Friendliness was Seth's secret weapon; it could disarm the most aggressive of grumps.

"Oh," Ma tittered, her free hand moving to her sallow cheek. "Yes, well. In future, perhaps you could

stink yourself up a bit before you come into the house; show a little disrespect."

"I'll try, Mrs M," Seth grinned, wiping his nose up his sleeve and making a show of rubbing it against the back of a dining chair. Ma nodded in tight-lipped approval.

"It's a start," she clipped.

Grandad floated down through the ceiling and into his armchair by the fire.

"Morning all. What a marvellous kerfuffle. It's been a while since we had a high alert."

Vendetta, noticing Seth for the first time, pointed one of her sausage fingers at him.

"Is he a Topsider?" she asked, aghast.

Ma blanched but was saved from further embarrassment by a loud crackling sound as Pa finally found the right station.

A voice filled the room and everyone fell silent to listen.

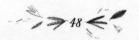

"We interrupt this broadcast to bring you a special Underland report. The Underland authorities have disclosed that the new Mayor of Underland, Ms Tardy Dawdle, has been ghostnapped! A letter of ransom has been received. The police have asked all Underlanders to remain extra vigilant at this time."

The ghosts, Topunders and a slightly perplexed Topsider were all frozen in shock; a ghostnap! Even a place as seemingly rambunctious and contrary as Underland had rules and regulations, boundaries of decency which simply weren't crossed. Ghostnapping was one of them. It was written in the Underland Constitution: *Statute 1A – No entity, dead or alive, may take a ghost against its will. Statute 1B – No entity, dead or alive, may hold a ghost captive against its will. Statute 1C – No entity, dead or alive, has the right to claim dominion over another entity's freedom, unless that entity has broken the laws of Underland.*

This was serious stuff indeed.

"Oh my gawd!" Ma was the first to break the silence. "I am shocked. Shocked to my bone marrow! My kidneys are all of a tremble!"

Then everyone began chattering loudly over everyone else.

"I can't believe it!"

"The nerve!"

"In this day and age!"

"Who would do such a thing?"

"The mayor of all ghosts! She's only been in office a month!"

Suddenly the room was filled with a wailing *OOOH AHHH OOOH AHHH OOOH AHHH* which seemed to split the air like thunder.

"What the…?" asked Seth, covering his ears.

"It's the Underland Police," Malice shouted over the noise.

With a finger firmly wedged in each ear, Malice looked out of the kitchen window. A veritable army

of police officers in long, shiny-buttoned coats and domed hats were running at full pelt up the garden. Seth had seen them too, his eyes growing rounder by the second.

"They must have come up through the Underland lift in the old oak tree!" Malice yelled.

The old oak tree in Felicity Square served as a gateway between Topside and Underland.

"What?" Seth shouted back.

OOOH AHHH OOOH AHHH OOOH AHHH

The siren was deafening; there was no room for anything else. It seemed to want to crawl in their ears and scoop their brains out.

By now, the others had spotted the police too. Vendetta was running around and around the kitchen, screeching and flapping her arms above her head with no apparent purpose. Animosity had dived under the table, while Pa tried to squeeze himself into a cupboard. Ma, still holding Antipathy-Rose, was

busily stuffing as much stolen swag as possible into her oversized bra. As a rule, Topunders tried to avoid all of the police forces all of the time. It was a fair bet that at any given moment a Topunder was probably partaking of something a bit iffy, and therefore it was sensible to keep a safe distance between them and the law. But right now, the law was closing in.

8

AN OPEN-AND-SHUT CASE

Malice didn't like the look of this situation one little bit. She looked around the kitchen and spotted a moth nibbling on the hearth rug. Still with her fingers in her ears, she knelt down beside it and whispered a request. She asked the moth to fly down to Underland, where Uncle Vex lived, and tell him that he was urgently needed at Malignant House. The moth fluttered its wings in agreement and flew out of the back door just as the police barged in.

Everyone froze where they were.

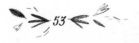

"'Ello 'ello 'ello!" said a portly officer with a handlebar moustache so pronounced it almost resembled mammoth tusks. "What 'ave we 'ere?"

Nobody said anything. The officer, who was clearly in charge, puffed his chest out like a proud pigeon and began to strut about the kitchen, his jowls wobbling with every step. Ordinarily, when ghosts are up in Topside their figures are indistinct, like a hologram; you can put your hand right through them. But the Underland Police had special powers which enabled them to interact physically with suspects when they were Topside. The portly policeman motioned to the other officers with a nod of his bulbous head, and they set about extracting the kitchen occupants from their various hiding places and lined them up in front of the hearth, even Seth, Malice and Grandad.

"Cat got your tongues, has it?" he asked, swaggering in front of them like a drunk uncle at a wedding. Malice got the impression he was enjoying

himself very much. "Well then, let *me* tell *you* what we 'ave 'ere. I am Chief Constable Braggart, the greatest mind the Underland police force has ever seen, and *you* are ghostnappers!"

Blustery bellows of shock and indignance ran up and down the line of Topunders.

"What the…?"

"Eh?"

"Who? Us?"

"Not me!"

"How dare you!"

"Utter nonsense!"

"Quiet down!" shouted Chief Braggart. He pointed at Vendetta and Animosity. "You two, sling yer hooks. It's the Maligns I'm after." He grinned wetly and licked his lips.

More gasps of surprise.

The Grudges were shoved towards the door.

"Don't you worry, Tetchy-Sue!" screeched

Vendetta. "We'll see this injustice put to rights!"

"Yeah!" shouted Animosity, shaking his fist. "We've got contacts!"

As the Grudges left the kitchen, Uncle Vex squeezed in past them. Malice had never been so pleased to see her uncle.

"Oh, not you!" sneered Chief Braggart.

Uncle Vex had clearly run all the way from the old oak tree and was panting, bent double trying to catch his breath.

"Sorry. Old. Girl," her uncle huffed, waving at Malice. "Got here. As soon. As. I. Could." From his bent-over position, he held out his hand to Chief Braggart. "Hello, Braggart. Still collaring the wrong people for the crime, I see!"

Chief Braggart's moustache quivered in outrage.

"Vexatious, you meddler! There's nothing for you 'ere; this is an open-and-shut case."

Uncle Vex, who had recovered his breath, stood

up straight and brushed himself down. He was the cleanest person Malice knew. His sharp suits – tailor-made on Underland's Shifty Row – were always perfectly pressed, and his hair was always gelled into a pristine quiff beneath his panama hat. For many years, Vexatious Malign's crime-fighting had brought shame upon the Malign family name and he and his brother – Pa – had been estranged because of it. But there had been a recent thawing in relations and Malice could tell Pa was pleased to have his younger brother back, even if he was a shocking do-gooder.

"Tell me, Braggart," said Uncle Vex, twiddling his cufflinks, "do you like arresting the wrong people or is it just a nasty habit?"

Chief Braggart's cheeks puffed out and his face turned bright red like a ripe tomato.

"Stay out of this, Vex. Officers cuff 'em!"

Ma quickly handed Antipathy-Rose to Malice before the police officers stepped towards Ma and

Pa and slapped handcuffs on their wrists.

"I am arresting you for the ghostnap of Mayor Tardy Dawdle. You have the right to remain silent. Anything you wish to say, I do not wish to hear."

Malice let out a little cry at seeing her parents in handcuffs and covered her mouth.

"We didn't do it!" screeched Ma.

"It's a frame-up!" bellowed Pa.

"Malice, my maggoty little fungus," Ma said tenderly. "We've been set up. You have to believe me!"

Malice ran to Ma and nestled in against her. She breathed in the comforting stink of *eau de skunk* that was her mother's signature scent. And Ma rested her face in her daughter's clean hair, even though the stench of shampoo made her retch.

"I do believe you, Ma," said Malice. "I really do."

And she did. Malice's parents were a lot of things, and none of them particularly palatable, but they were always honest about their dishonesty.

"We've been framed, my girl," Pa said, his bottom lip quivering with emotion. "Our fate is in your hands; you've always had more brains than buffoonery. Make it right, Malice. Make it right."

"I'll try, Pa," said Malice.

"You can do it, Malice," said Ma. "Gawd knows you're a disappointment in the mischief department, but you're one heck of a detective. You take after your grandad." Ma did an approximation of a smile at Grandad and Malice. Ma's smiles were rare, and when she did bestow one upon you, it was like watching a hyena growling – but to Malice it was deeply comforting.

Grandad drifted over and rested a ghostly arm around Ma's shoulders.

"We'll put our heads together and sort this bloomin' mess out," he said soothingly, and for once Ma didn't moan about them doing too much thinking.

"Ahem," Pa cleared his throat and addressed Uncle

Vex. "I wouldn't normally stoop so low, little bro, but I must ask you to h-h-h-help Malice clear our names."

Pa looked as uncomfortable saying it as Uncle Vex looked unnerved at hearing it. As a rule, Maligns didn't do helping; they certainly didn't ask for it. Helping was not considered a worthwhile pursuit unless you were helping yourself to someone else's property.

"Of course I will, old chum," Uncle Vex was visibly moved. "Goes without saying. You didn't even need to ask."

"I wish I'd known," Pa grumbled. "I hate the *H*-word."

"You too, Seth," added Ma. "You're a strange little floppy haired do-gooder, and you stink of fabric softener, but you know your way around a mystery."

Seth's cheeks were rosy with pride.

"Thanks, Mrs Malign," he gushed. "I won't let you down."

"See that you don't," sniffed Ma.

"Right, that's enough of the cosy heart-to-heart stuff!" Chief Braggart blustered. "Let's get these miscreants down to the station."

Malice stepped forward.

"Have you found the mayor?" she asked.

Chief Braggart glared.

"Not yet. But now we've got our culprits, it's only a matter of time. A couple of nights in the dungeons oughta loosen their tongues."

"And what is your evidence against my parents?"

Chief Braggart laughed smugly.

"A certain bejewelled cutlass was found at the scene of the crime. The very same cutlass Tetchy-Sue used to rob that Topside jewellers. Is that evidence enough for you, little girl?"

Malice glared at him.

"I wondered where that had got to," said Ma. "I thought you'd taken it for the Pirate Treasure display in the bathroom, Pa."

"And I thought you'd taken it for the Medieval display in the orangery," said Pa.

"So, someone took it," said Malice.

"And planted it at the scene to incriminate them!" said Grandad.

"But why would anyone want to?" Chief Braggart asked sarcastically. "What with the Maligns being so popular and all."

"Someone's stitched us up, proper," said Ma to Malice.

"I know, Ma."

"Look after your sister. There's an old lawnmower in the shed she can chew on if she gets cranky."

"Don't worry, Ma. I'll take care of everything."

Ma swooped down and kissed Malice on the top of her head and whispered "my brilliant girl" in her ear. Malice felt her heart swell. She was often at odds with her parents' way of life but the love was never in question.

"Take 'em away!" Chief Braggart roared gleefully. He turned to Ma and Pa.

"Ghostnapping the mayor of Underland? I wouldn't be surprised if they locked you up and threw away the key!"

"But the All Hallows' Haunt is in two days," Ma protested. "We're the hosts!"

"Not any more you're not," Chief Braggart chuckled. "Your hosting privilege has been rescinded. Mordacious and Truculent MacNe'erdoowell will throw the ball instead. I'll have my officers contact them at once."

"Nooooooooooooooooooooooooooooooooooooo!" Ma wailed, as she and Pa were escorted off the Malign premises and across to the old oak tree in the square.

Had the residents of Felicity Square looked out of their windows at that moment, all they would have seen was Ma and Pa walking in handcuffs, quite

alone. They wouldn't have seen the ghostly police officers crowded around them, or Chief Braggart striding confidently ahead of them like a hairy plum pudding on legs. And once they'd slipped out of view behind the old oak tree, they wouldn't have seen a door slide open in the trunk and a bellboy waiting in the lift to take them down to the land of the dead, and the dungeons of Underland.

BEING DEAD CAN GET
A BIT BORING

Malice stood, stunned. Seth sidled over and gave her a comforting shoulder barge.

"Never a dull moment in your house, is there?" he said.

"No," Malice sighed. "Sometimes I think a bit of dull would be quite nice."

"Don't worry, Malice. We'll get them back."

"Absolutely!" joined in Uncle Vex. "No need for the long face, old girl. Never in my wildest nightmares did

I ever think I'd say these words, but I do believe that Ma and Pa are…" He paused here at the incongruity of what he was about to say. "*Innocent!* The more I think about it, the more strongly I feel it. All we have to do is prove it."

"You're right!" said Malice, setting her sister down and letting her toddle around the kitchen. "We should approach this like any other case. We need to fact-find and gather intel."

"Maybe we should compile a list of people who don't like your parents," suggested Seth.

Malice and Uncle Vex looked at each other and grimaced.

"That might be a long list," said Malice.

"OK then, let's make a list of all the people who *do* like your parents," Seth said brightly.

66

"That would be a much shorter list," said Uncle Vex.

"You're pretty much looking at them," Malice added.

She'd never really thought about it before, but it was true. On the face of it, Ma and Pa seemed incredibly hard to like. You had to really know them to love them and hardly anybody really knew them. *What a sad thing*, she thought to herself.

"How does one attempt to prove the innocence of two people who have made it their business to always be guilty of something?" asked Uncle Vex.

"We find the real culprits," said Malice simply, as if this was the easiest thing in the world.

"Maybe if we could find the mayor, she could be a witness for your parents, you know, tell the police it wasn't them," said Seth.

"Yes! And her evidence would be a great help in tracking down the real ghostnappers," agreed Malice. After the initial shock, her Malign tenacity was

returning; she could feel the cogs in her mind beginning to turn. "Now, where would someone hide a mayor?" she asked herself, tapping her chin.

"Ah, well, there I may be able to help," Uncle Vex piped up. "As soon as I got your moth-message, I fired off a ghoulagram to one of my contacts down at the police station. I'd heard about the ghostnap on the radio and I asked her to send me a copy of the ransom note. She said she'd send it via moth-mail. It should be here any minute ... in fact..."

A sound like the pages of many books being turned very fast drifted up through the floorboards, quickly followed by a cluster of Underland moths. Their wings were thin and delicate as cobwebs, colourless and dry, as though if you touched them they would crumble to nothing. The cluster moved as one to Malice. She held out her hands and the moths delivered their cargo into them. A note. A ransom note.

Malice thanked the moths and they fluttered up to the attic for a well-earned nibble on Grandad's throw blankets; moths were always welcome in Grandad's attic.

"What does it say, duck?" asked Grandad.

Some of the more curious ancestors from the mausoleum had floated over to join them in the kitchen. Ghosts loved gossip and there wasn't a whole lot of excitement in the mausoleum. They settled themselves in, some sitting on and around the table, some laying along the tops of cupboards or on the worktops – much to the consternation of the kitchen ghosts – and waited, excited anticipation in their translucent eyes.

Malice smoothed the note out and laid it on the table. She cleared her throat and read out loud.

Over Underland and six-feet under, in a place to forget, in a dingy rotunda, sits Mayor Dawdle, all alone in her bunker.

Unless you agree to my foul proposition, I'll not feel inclined to divulge her position.

Bring me the keys to the Underland Bank, the codes to the vault and the use of a tank.

Leave the keys in a boat at the pier on Bone River, your mayor is at risk if you do not deliver.

I'll give you one night to fulfil my demands, after that it's your fault if the mayor comes to harm.

Extraction of loot is a lonesome vocation, so make yourselves scarce to avoid agitation.

The fate of the mayor rests on how you proceed, will she be rescued or abandoned for greed?

The clock's started ticking, it's time to engage, or leave her to languish in a windowless cage.

End of the line or start of a quest, be wise and adhere to this villain's behest.

"Well, really!" exclaimed Lady Insidious. "By all means, heckle her during speeches, throw rotten tomatoes at her if you must, smoosh a pie in her face if you really feel the need, but one simply does not ghostnap the mayor."

"Quite right, dear," agreed Lady Munificence. "It simply isn't done in impolite society."

"Don't *dear* me, you goody-two-shoes!" snapped Lady Insidious. "Go boil your head!"

Lady Munificence was unpopular amongst the Malign ancestors for having given the family fortune away to the poor.

"Well, according to that ransom note, it has been very much *done*," said Grandad, trying to steer the conversation back to the matter in hand, "and Ma and Pa are the chief suspects."

"Except they didn't do it," said Malice.

"Classic scapeghost situation," mused Magnanimous Malign.

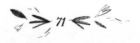

Malice was rereading the note.

"What is it, duck?" asked Grandad.

Malice chewed her lip.

"I don't know," she mused. "Something about it doesn't feel right."

"Is it because neither Ma nor Pa have the creative writing skills to write a rhyming ransom note?" asked Uncle Vex.

"No, although you do have a point. It's something about the way it's written."

"Ransom notes rarely make comfortable reading," said Uncle Vex.

"It's almost as though they're laying down the gauntlet, challenging us," Malice mused.

"All I see is a list of delicious threats," said Lady Insidious.

"But why give us all these clues to where the mayor has been taken?" Malice persisted.

Seth looked at the note again.

"I see what you mean," he agreed. "Surely it would be in their best interests *not* to give us any information that could help with her discovery?"

"I agree with the two young do-gooders," said Marauder, straightening her face covering. Marauder had been an infamous highwaywoman. "Back when I was alive, in my kidnapping days, I wouldn't have dreamed of giving clues to my victims' locations. What would be the point in that? It was a heist, not a blooming scavenger hunt!"

"Are you suggesting that the kidnappers *want* the mayor to be found?" scoffed Uncle Vex.

"I am suggesting that we should consider the possibility," said Malice. "After all, when has anything in Underland ever been exactly as it seems?"

"On that, we are agreed." Her uncle nodded sagely.

"In that case, we had better start unpicking this ransom note for clues," said Grandad.

"Doesn't anyone in Underland ever just write a normal, straightforward note, without rhymes or puzzles?" asked Seth.

All eyes – dead and alive – turned in his direction.

"What," Lady Insidious addressed him haughtily, "would be the point in that?"

Purloin Malign observed Seth distastefully.

"Clearly, *you've* never been dead!" he sneered. "Because if you had been, you'd know better."

"Er, sorry?" said Seth.

"It's not so much that they *can't* write a straightforward note," Uncle Vex explained. "It's more that, after a couple of hundred years or so, being dead can get a bit boring, so the ghosts like to mix things up a bit – keep the old synapses snapping."

"That makes sense," said Seth. "I really do enjoy the riddles," he added placatingly, smiling really hard at the sea of mean faces glaring in his direction.

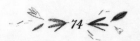

"Of course you do," smiled Magnanimous kindly. Magnanimous was another Malign ancestor for whom the mischief-making gene had been absent. He too was unpopular with his fellow ghosts in the mausoleum.

"And we appreciate your help with our little Underland mysteries," added Lady Munificence. She laid a chilly hand on Seth's arm and, although she couldn't actually touch him, her nearness caused his skin to jump instantly into goosebumps. He smiled through it; ghosts got upset if you flinched away from their touch.

"Oh, both of you, boil your heads!" snapped Lady Insidious. "In fact, if you keep on with this incessant niceness, I'll boil them for you!"

"I'll help!" added Merciless Malign.

Grandad clapped his hands; the sound of it was like wind buffeting loose window shutters, and it echoed around the kitchen, silencing the bickering ghosts.

"Enough!" he said. "This ransom note is the best and only clue we've got to help us find the mayor and prove Ma and Pa's innocence. If you're not going to help, go back to your tombs."

The ancestors pulled faces but stayed quiet. Everyone leaned over the note and began to quietly unpick the contents.

"Let's start with descriptions," said Malice, chewing the top of her pencil.

"*Six feet under*," Uncle Vex mused. "A grave, perhaps? It says it's above Underland, so she must be Topside."

"There are a lot of graveyards Topside," said Grandad. "It would take us years to check every one."

"What's a rotunda?" asked Seth.

"It's a building, or a room in a building, which is round," Uncle Vex replied.

"So, the mayor is in a round underground room," said Seth thoughtfully.

At these words, Malice's stomach began to squirm with unease. She took a deep breath and tried to ignore the prickling heat in her cheeks, while she kept deciphering the note. *A windowless cage,* she thought to herself. *It couldn't be, could it?*

The kitchen rang with shouted suggestions from the ghosts of where Mayor Dawdle might be being held.

"Buried beneath a circus big top!" shouted one.

"I'll bet she's in one of those secret underground bunkers left over from the war," said another.

"Or the London Underground," suggested Marauder. "The tube tunnels are round and windowless; dingy too, late at night."

"By Cockroaches!" exclaimed Uncle Vex. "You could be on to something there, Marauder."

"Malice, ducky, have you noticed anything about the layout of the note?" asked Grandad. "There's something about it I can't quite put my finger on."

"You can't put your finger on anything," sniffed Lady Insidious. "You're dead!"

"Now, now," soothed Lady Munificence. "Let's try to be charitable, shall we?"

"Put a sock in it, you traitorous do-gooder!" the other lady retorted.

Malice trained her eyes to look at the note from a different angle. She studied the rhythm of the note and checked vertically and diagonally for patterns in the text.

"It could be an acrostic poem," she suggested.

"An a-what's-it?" asked a ghost with his head tucked neatly under his arm; Stinkard Malign had had an unfortunate encounter with a guillotine in 1782.

"An acrostic poem is when the first letters of each sentence can be put together to form a word," Malice replied. She turned to a fresh page in her notebook – Malice never went anywhere without her trusty notebook in her pocket – and began to jot down the

78

letters. With each new letter she wrote, the squirming unease in her stomach became more pronounced.

OUBLIETTE

"Oh my!" said Uncle Vex. "Oh me, oh my!"

10

WE'RE IN THIS TOGETHER

Malice gave a nervous little laugh.

"Oubliette." Grandad read the word out loud and gave a long whistle.

"There must be hundreds, thousands even, of oubliettes in Underland," Malice reasoned.

"But the poem states that the mayor isn't being held in Underland," said Grandad, rubbing a ghostly hand over his ghostly beard.

"What's an oubliette?" asked Seth.

"It's a windowless underground dungeon," Malice sighed.

"From the French word *oublier*, which means to forget. Prisoners would be thrown into oubliettes and forgotten about. Which neatly ties in with the first sentence in the ransom note 'in a place to forget.'" added Uncle Vex.

"Cool!" Seth grinned, and then upon seeing Malice's expression his grin faltered and he added, "Not cool?"

"We have an oubliette in Malignant House," she explained. "Ma and Pa use it as a kind of holding cell while they're waiting to approve new haunting ghosts for their Topside haunting houses."

Seth's mouth dropped open.

"But I am quite sure it's all just a coincidence and this ransom note refers to another oubliette entirely," Malice said, smiling too brightly. "Quite, quite sure.

Really, really sure."

"Who you trying to convince?" asked Marauder. "Us, or yourself?"

"The thing is, dearest niece," Uncle Vex said softly, "Ma and Pa are extremely fond of loot, and if there's one thing the Underland Bank vaults contain in spades it's, well, loot." He shrugged his shoulders and the shoulder pads in his sharp suit jutted out like two landing pads for stag beetles.

"But they wouldn't…" Malice glanced about the kitchen and was greeted with sceptical expressions. "Yes, they like loot but they're mischief-makers, not ghostnappers! And it wouldn't make any sense. They've waited years to host the All Hallows' Haunt, they wouldn't jeopardize that … would they?"

"There's only one way to find out," said Grandad.

Malice went to pick up Antipathy-Rose, whose lips were black from all the coal she'd nibbled in the coal scuttle. Her little sister was now on her tippy toes

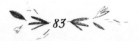

busily throwing things over the fire guard into the fire and giggling as they burned. She clapped her hands as one of her teddies went up in flames. Looking around for more things to incinerate, Antipathy-Rose came upon a piece of folded paper near the grate. But just as she was about to drop it into the flames, Malice swept her up into her arms and the paper fell just shy of the hungry fire, singeing at the corners in the heat. Malice caught sight of it, but it didn't properly catch her attention until a set of digits and letters began to appear on the paper. She reached down, still holding her sister, and plucked the paper from the hearth. As she inspected it, the characters faded and the paper was blank once more. Ordinarily this would have piqued her curiosity, but right now she had bigger things to worry about than disappearing letters. All the same, she popped it in her pinafore pocket for later inspection.

The motley mass of ghouls and mortals hurried down ramshackle galleries and dusty corridors. With each new turn the ceilings became lower, the lighting dimmer and the walkways narrower, as though the walls were squeezing in against them.

Malice didn't often come to this part of the house. This was where her parents did most of their Underland business; it was a place of shady dealings and odious machinations. The air was dank. The peeling wallpaper which furnished the rest of the house was absent here. They were surrounded by cold, stone walls and the tinny *clink clink* of water dripping from the ceiling. Antipathy-Rose buried her head into Malice's shoulder and tightened her arms around her neck.

"It's OK, Anti," Malice soothed. "There's nothing to worry about." But in her head, she was reciting a

silent mantra over and over again. *Please don't let it be our oubliette! Please don't let it be our oubliette!*

The ghosts which her parents hired for hauntings were not a friendly bunch – another reason for Malice to steer clear of this part of the house. They mostly came from the Haunting Quarter, where all the most unpleasant ghouls resided. The oubliette prevented the haunting ghosts from getting loose in Topside before Ma and Pa had vetted them properly. Renting out properties to ghosts was lucrative but it came with certain responsibilities which had to be strictly adhered to.

Though she had never seen it, Malice knew that the oubliette lay in the floor of Ma's office. Malice half hoped the door would be locked when she tried the handle, but no such luck – the door swung open.

A large cupboard stood against the far wall; a cold breeze that she didn't have time to think about right now whistled out through the keyhole. There was

a mahogany desk piled high with papers, and the cracked leather chair which sat beside it had seen better days. Filing cabinets with drawers pulled open and folders spilling out were dotted about the room.

"How … cosy," gulped Uncle Vex, pulling his suit jacket tighter around him as though it could shield him from the hooded eyes which stared out from the portraits on the walls.

But Malice couldn't tear her gaze away from a lump beneath the threadbare rug in the middle of the room, which she assumed was covering the trapdoor. She was torn between wanting to heave the hatch open to get it over with and not wanting to look at all. What would she do if the mayor was down there? If her own parents were ghostnappers? Sure, they were smelly and dirty and mischievous, but in a lovable sort of way. She didn't want to discover that Ma and Pa partook of such nefarious dealings – she'd rather not know.

Uncle Vex cast the rug aside, coughing on the cloud of dust that rose up from it. Malice froze. As if sensing her discomfort, Grandad, Seth and Uncle Vex closed ranks around her.

"Whatever happens," said Seth, "we're in this together."

"Oh, the mayor won't be down there," Malice trilled brightly. "I expect we'll find some ghastly ghoul or other waiting to be let loose on the Topsiders."

She gave a nervous little laugh and smiled a bit too widely. Seth tried to match her smile with his own, but it didn't quite meet his eyes.

"Come on then, Vexatious. Show us all your muscles and lift the trapdoor," said Grandad.

The ancestors grinned viciously and drew closer. Uncle Vex made a show of pulling up his sleeves and reluctantly grabbed hold of the iron ring in the centre of the hatch. He heaved at it once, twice, three times; a little bead of sweat dripped from his perfectly coiffed

quiff and on to one of his shiny shoes. With a groan, the trapdoor opened. And a small voice from far, far below called out:

"Hello?"

11

MY GUTS WILL NEVER
LET ME DOWN

Mayor Tardy Dawdle blinked in the dim light
as her eyes roamed around Ma's office.
She was perched on a barrel of smuggled
whisky, leftover from the 1740s, with one
of Grandad's armchair blankets draped
around her shoulders. Uncle Vex had
asked the ghosts, who'd crowded in
around her like overeager tourists,
to give her some space.

While Uncle Vex took the lead with gentle questions, Malice stood a little way back nervously chewing her fingernails. She couldn't believe it. She *wouldn't* believe it! She wondered what this meant for her family; the Underland authorities took a dim view of ghostnapping. Surely there was some mistake? She knew what it looked like. The evidence seemed overwhelming, like there was no other possible explanation than that her parents were guilty. But could they really have done such a thing?

Malice's brain bulged with questions and her heart was fat with sorrow and disappointment.

"You know your parents better than anyone, Malice," said Seth quietly. He had a way of knowing just what Malice was thinking. "My dads always say I should trust my gut feeling because my guts will never let me down. What do your guts tell you?"

Malice breathed deeply and closed her eyes. She searched inside herself – past what the evidence

showed and what her brain told her, past what she wanted to believe – and into her very core, the place where true things were felt. That place where you know in your bones when something feels right or wrong. And in Malice's bones she knew that despite what it looked like on the outside, her parents would never do anything that would take them away from her and her sister; mischief was their livelihood, but family was their life.

She opened her eyes and looked at Seth.

"My guts tell me that Ma and Pa wouldn't risk losing us."

Seth smiled and nodded.

"Then that's the truth of it," he said.

Malice smiled back at her bestie.

"Just tell us what you remember." Uncle Vex was trying to coax information from the bedraggled, befuddled mayor.

The mayor shivered. She was a slight ghost, with

small, round glasses perched on the kind of face which would always be ready to listen or to offer a cup of stinging-nettle tea. Her tweed jacket and matching skirt were crumpled but smart, despite all her jacket buttons being done up wrong as though she'd been in a frightful hurry. Her glorious afro was pulled up into a sort of messy bun which looked as though it had been attacked by a strong wind and no amount of hairslides and clips could contain it. She had the air of a woman who was perpetually running late for something.

"I'm afraid I don't remember very much really," she began in a small voice. "One minute I was signing some papers in my office and the next I was grabbed from behind. They put a sack over my head and the rest is a bit of a blur. I didn't know where I was!"

Uncle Vex twiddled his quiff as he pondered.

"Can you tell us anything about your ghostnapper?" he asked.

Mayor Dawdle shrugged.

"There were two of them: a woman and a man. Quite stinky. The woman seemed to be in charge."

All heads, ghostly and otherwise, swivelled to look at Marauder Malign. The highwaywoman baulked.

"Oh no!" she snapped. "You're not pinning this on me. Not my style, me hearties. I never grabbed no one, and I certainly didn't put bags on their heads. My kidnaps were civilized affairs. Ladies of the time were queuing up to be kidnapped by me so they could boast about their adventures at society balls; I made captivity captivating!"

Grandad addressed Mayor Dawdle next.

"Pardon me, your dishonourable worshipness, but, in your opinion, would you say that it was Tetchy-

Sue and Pugnacious Malign who kidnapped you?"

Mayor Dawdle shrugged her shoulders and gave them each an apologetic look.

"I'm sorry," she said. "I'd like to be able to tell you one way or the other, but I really don't know. It could have been them, but it could just have easily not been them at all. It was dark and I was disorientated. I can tell you this, though, one of them started my allergies off; I almost sneezed my own brains out!"

Uncle Vex opened his mouth to ask the mayor some more questions but was cut short by a rumbling beneath their feet which began as a vibration and quickly became a tremor, growing swiftly in volume.

"What's happening?" asked Malice.

"Is it an earthquake?" Seth shouted over the noise.

The doors of the large cupboard began to judder. The wood rippled under the force of something behind it. The banging grew louder and louder and louder until with a crash the doors blew open and

96

a ghost dressed as an old town crier burst through them. He brought with him a cold wind and a flurry of snow.

12

THE PERFECT WAY TO FRAME MY PARENTS

The gaggle who were gathered in Ma's office stood open-mouthed as the ghost straightened his tricorn hat and unrolled a scroll from which he began to read in a very loud voice.

"Hear ye, hear ye!" he began. "The case of Mayor Tardy Dawdle's ghostnap is to be heard at the Underland Public Courts. Pugnacious and Tetchy-Sue Malign stand accused of the crime. The case will convene at one o'clock sharp. All welcome. Bring

your own snacks."

And with that, he stepped back into the cupboard and the doors slammed shut behind him.

Malice's stomach scrunched with nerves. This was all happening very quickly. She'd expected to have more time to get her head around this mystery. They'd rescued the mayor but had no proof that her parents weren't guilty. There was no question that Malice wouldn't be at that hearing; she simply had to be. The others, however, seemed more interested in the town crier's mode of transport than his message.

"Well, I'll be…" said Uncle Vex in wonderment. He opened the doors to the cupboard, peeped inside, letting in another icy gust, and then closed them again. "I haven't seen one of these in years. I thought they'd all been closed in the great portal overhaul of 1880. Did you know this was here?" he looked at Grandad.

Grandad shook his head.

"I didn't realize it was still in use. I don't come down this end of the house."

Uncle Vex turned his questioning gaze on Malice, who shrugged her shoulders.

"I've only been in here a couple of times, and then only for a few seconds. Ma says it's dangerous in this part of the house. To be honest, I just thought it was a wardrobe for her coats – she has a lot of coats."

"What's so special about it?" asked Seth.

"It's a private portal. The Underland council scrapped all private portals to Underland in Topunder homes in the late nineteeth Century," Uncle Vex began. "There'd been a spate of Topsiders accidentally stumbling upon them at parties and the like, and being transported to Underland. You can imagine how that went down! In the end, it was decided that portals in private homes were too risky and they were outlawed in 1880. Very few remained, and they had to be policed to ensure that only Topunders came in

and out of them."

"More to the point," Malice began, "it means that someone could have kidnapped Mayor Dawdle and deposited her in our oubliette without anyone else seeing. The perfect way to frame my parents."

"Unless your parents are guilty!" sneered Lady Insidious.

"Haven't you got a tomb to go to?" snapped Grandad.

Lady Insidious narrowed her eyes at Grandad, but Magnanimous nodded his head.

"I think we should *all* probably get back to the mausoleum and let the investigators investigate," he said. "I am sorry to say that thus far our presence has not brought much to the party in terms of helping our successors."

The ancestors grumbled but grudgingly agreed and began drifting out of Ma's office. Marauder said she'd left some entrails bubbling on the stove which

needed stirring anyway. Merciless Malign said he had to get back as he was expecting a parcel from eSlay, and Lady Insidious had an appointment with her plague doctor and she couldn't hang around here all day.

When the others were out of earshot, Lady 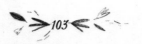 Munificence stopped halfway through the wall and whispered, "If you need our help for anything at all, just send us a moth-message." Then she winked and was gone.

The office felt less chilly without the ancestors. Mayor Dawdle had recovered from her shock and seemed almost perky. Malice looked at her watch.

"Do you think this portal is an illegal one?" Malice asked.

Uncle Vex rubbed his chin.

"I'm not sure. The town crier used it, which would suggest it was a legal portal, but equally, the town criers of Underland have to cover a lot of areas quickly and they aren't overly picky about the legality of their transportation."

"I once saw a town crier lie flat on the roof of a carriage to hitch a free ride to his next location," added Grandad.

Uncle Vex was still thinking. "I suppose Ma and Pa could have got special permission because of the Haunting Agency. There'll be guards at the top and bottom if it's an authorized portal. Why do you ask?"

"I was just thinking that it's half past twelve now, and we need to be at Ma and Pa's court hearing at one o'clock. We could deliver the mayor back at the same time—"

"Oh, yes please!" cut in Mayor Dawdle.

"This portal would be mighty handy. And perhaps, Mayor Dawdle, you wouldn't mind telling the authorities that you couldn't identify your ghostnappers? It might help my parents," Malice finished.

"I will tell them the truth," said the mayor. "And do call me Tardy. I will tell them that my captors could have been anyone – there will be no finger pointing from me."

"Thank you," said Malice.

"Can I suggest we hold off from informing the authorities that the mayor has been found? Just for the time being?" asked Uncle Vex. "It might be our best chance of trapping the real culprits. If their intention is to frame your parents and they think that the mayor is still safely ensconced in the oubliette, they will continue to drop clues to the police. All we have to do is follow the breadcrumbs back to where the clues are coming from."

Malice chewed her lip, unconvinced.

"I understand your concerns," Uncle Vex continued. "But as it stands, it's not going to look very good for your parents when the police find out that the mayor was in *their* oubliette. This will buy us

more time to crack the case."

Malice puffed out a breath.

"I suppose you're right," she said. "What do you think, Tardy?"

"Oh, I think it's wonderfully exciting! Sneaking around, pretending not to be here; what an absolute hoot!"

Mayor Dawdle really was an awfully good sport. Malice hoped this plan didn't backfire.

"OK," said Malice. "We need to get to the courthouse and this portal, legal or not, is the quickest way to get to Underland. It seems silly not to use it."

"She makes a good point," said Grandad.

Uncle Vex licked two fingers and smoothed his eyebrows thoughtfully.

"Fair enough," he agreed, "Since time is of the essence. Seth, have you got your Underland Pass?"

Seth pulled a lanyard out of his pocket and put it around his neck. A Topsider in Underland was

fair game for any nefarious ghost or cantankerous ghoul. Seth's lanyard was proof that he was under Uncle Vex's protection and therefore no ghostly fiends would mess with him. It basically meant he was bullyproof, something which Malice often wished they were at school.

"Just out of interest, what would happen if this were an unauthorized portal?" asked Seth.

"Um, it's pretty straightforward really," said Uncle Vex casually. "If we were caught using it, we'd be arrested and thrown into jail."

"Oh, is that all?" Seth replied, with more than a hint of sarcasm.

13

NOBODY LIKES
SKINNED KNUCKLES

Uncle Vex opened the doors to the cupboard again,
standing aside and ushering everyone in.

"Now, I'm not exactly sure what form this portal
takes, so if you could all just wait for me, I'll see what
we're dealing with," he said.

Malice, still holding her sister, looked around.
It was a small, cold, cave-like room, dimly lit with
candles in sconces on three walls. Instead of a fourth
wall, the floor dropped away sharply into what looked

like an ice-covered slide, which twisted down and away into a dark hole. There was fresh snow on the ground below their feet and more snow was puffing upwards from out of the abyss in white fluffy flakes which fluttered down on to their heads.

"It's snowing upwards!" exclaimed Seth.

"Yes, it does that when it can't snow downwards," said Grandad, pointing to the curved stone ceiling above their heads.

The doors to the cupboard clicked shut behind them and Uncle Vex plucked a flaming torch from a sconce on the wall and came to stand with them. He peeped over the edge of the slide and nodded in quiet confirmation.

"It's old school all right," he said. "This is a classic 1827 sledge portal. It's essentially an ice helter-skelter: super-fast, super-efficient."

At that moment the snow banked-up in the far corner, shivered and fell away as a slender ghost in a

skirt suit, with square glasses and two icicles holding her bun in place, sat up and demanded, "Dead or alive? You must declare your bodily state before using this portal."

Uncle Vex, completely unflustered by the previously snow-buried ghost, did a quick headcount and replied, "Umm that'll be three living Topunders, one living Topsider, and two very dead ghosts, please."

The woman scribbled down their details in her folder and then lay back down in the snow.

"You may pass," she said, before adding, "you couldn't just cover me over a bit, could you? It took me ages to bury myself last time."

"Of course!" Uncle Vex replied obligingly and began to heap snow over the prostrate ghost until she was completely obscured. "Now..."he began to look around the small cave, shining his torch into the far corners until he spied what he was looking for. "Aha!"

He dragged a magazine rack into view, which held,

instead of magazines, large round tea trays painted with flowers and fruit. He handed a tray each to Seth and Malice. Since Grandad and Mayor Dawdle were ghosts, they didn't need a tea tray – they wouldn't be solid until they reached Underland.

"Now, whatever you do, don't put your hands out," Uncle Vex warned. "Nobody likes skinned knuckles!"

Malice gulped and wondered how she was going to keep a hold of Antipathy-Rose and stay upright on a tea-tray sledge on an ice helter-skelter.

"Is this dangerous?" Malice asked. "This feels dangerous. I'm not sure we should be doing…" But her reservations were cut off by Seth's cry of "Weeeeeeeeeeeeeeeeeee!" as the top of his blond head disappeared from view and he sailed off down the slide at top speed on his tea tray.

"This is brilliant!" his voice echoed back to Malice.

"Right, well, that settles that then," she said.

Malice sat herself on the tea tray, with her sister

on her lap, and pulled her knees up to secure her. Beside her, Uncle Vex was readying himself as well. Mayor Dawdle and Grandad held hands and dived headfirst off the edge. Their screeches of delight echoed back up to where Malice and her uncle had shuffled themselves to the top of the slide.

"See you in Underland." Uncle Vex grinned. "Last one to the bottom is a rotten egg."

"That'll be you then," said Malice, and Antipathy-Rose giggled in agreement. With the briefest look at the steep drop, she pulled her sister tighter to her and tipped them both over the edge.

The ride down was fast, but the snow was soft and cushiony as they bounced along at speed, twisting around and around the deep corkscrew curves. Antipathy-Rose's squeals of delight rang in Malice's ears and despite all her worries, Malice couldn't help but join in. Her hair flew out behind her and the candles on the walls melded into two long orange

spirals as she whooshed passed them. Behind her, Uncle Vex was screaming in a high-pitched voice and Malice laughed, leaning forwards on her tea tray to propel them faster; she was no rotten egg.

As the bottom came into view, the slide grew wider and tapered out into a gentler decline and Malice slowed enough to see Seth leaning smugly against a sign which read, *Please return your tea tray here.* An older gentleman, wearing a khaki-coloured World War One army uniform, stood nearby, fast asleep, holding an open book and fountain pen poised to make notes.

As the sisters' tea tray came to a stop with a gentle *Pshhhhhh* in a bank of snow, Grandad came over and took Antipathy-Rose from Malice so she could get up.

Antipathy-Rose was delighted – what with Grandad being a ghost and all, cuddles were only possible when he was in Underland territory where his form became solid like a living person's. All ghosts in Underland were solid.

"Fun, huh!" said Seth, taking Malice's tea tray from her and replacing it.

"I had my reservations, but it actually was," Malice agreed.

The gently snoring soldier awoke with a snort and shouted, "State your name and business!"

"Malice Morbid Malign," Malice said, watching the soldier write it down in his book. "I'm here to attend my parents court hearing."

"Very good! As you were!" he barked and promptly fell back to sleep, still standing, pen poised for the next entrant.

"Not much of a security guard," whispered Seth.

"I wonder if he recorded who came through

yesterday in his book?" Malice said, inching closer to the sleeping soldier. She peeped over at the open book, running her eyes over the lists of names and dates, but there was nothing recorded at all for yesterday. "Dung beetles!" Malice swore under her breath.

"I don't suppose it would be too hard to sneak past him," said Seth, just as the soldier woke again and shouted, "Name and business!" at no one in particular, before snuffling and letting his head nod. Seth and Malice shared a look.

Uncle Vex was still screaming as he came around the last bend. Unlike Malice, he didn't appear to have slowed at all and he sailed straight past them, shrieking, and crashed into the buffers. The buffers were made from hundreds of eyeless, dismembered soft toys and teddies which induced further terrified caterwauling from her uncle. Malice and Seth rushed to help him up.

"Exhilarating, what!" said Uncle Vex, stretching his

legs. "To the untrained ear I may have sounded like I was screaming with fear but those are in fact the noises I make when I am enjoying the thrill of an adrenaline rush." He looked to the side and found a teddy bear's leg – from the buffers – resting on his shoulder and began to scream, high and shrill, jumping and swatting at it, squeaking, "Get it off! Get it off me!"

Malice swatted at it.

"It's off," she said, directing his gaze to the limb sticking out of the snow.

Uncle Vex straightened his tie and smoothed his quiff.

"Was that the sound of another exhilarating adrenaline rush?" asked Seth.

Malice stifled a laugh, and even Mayor Dawdle had to hide a snigger.

"Nobody likes a smarty-pants!" Uncle Vex replied haughtily.

The soldier still hadn't woken to record Uncle Vex's

name and business in his logbook, further cementing Malice's belief that it wouldn't have been hard for the ghostnappers to sneak past the portal guard.

"That was better than any ride I've ever been on," said Seth, looking longingly at the helter-skelter.

"It reminds me of when our governess fixed a builders' rubbish chute to the top turret of Malignant House and threw Pugnacious and I down it." Uncle Vex got a faraway look about him and said fondly, "Ah, the folly of childhood; Mother playing frisbee with us using her Ninja throwing stars and Father chasing us around the lawn on his motorbike with a jousting stick. Golden memories."

"I think I would have liked growing up with your parents," Seth said to Uncle Vex, and Malice rolled her eyes at him.

"Well, of course, we didn't have games consoles and mobile phones in those days," said Uncle Vex.

Malice was about to interject that *she* didn't have

those things either, when Uncle Vex let out another ear-busting yowl.

"What is it?" asked Malice, alarmed. "Are you hurt?"

Uncle Vex looked desolate.

"Some of the paint from the tea tray has transferred on to my suit!" he whined. "I just picked this up from Madame Suture this week."

Malice tutted and took a look. Sure enough, the back of his trousers was covered in paint splodges.

She shrugged.

"Could be worse," she said.

"'Could be worse'?" he lamented. "'Could be worse'? This is a one of a kind!"

"It is now," muttered Seth.

"Shall we get going?" Malice asked, conscious of the time. Uncle Vex's passion for fashion could be all consuming.

"Yes!" said Uncle Vex. "We have a courtroom to gatecrash, let us hurry forth!"

PEEPING PORTRAITS AND JIU-JITSU MASTERS

The only way out of the portal was through an iron door with a circular handwheel, not dissimilar to what you might expect to find in a submarine. Uncle Vex had recently had a manicure, so Malice and Seth heaved at the wheel together. After several turns there came the ticking clack of many cogs turning and, with a sigh, the heavy door swished open on to Underland.

The glow-worms busily squiggling in the earthen sky above pulsed out a muted light which bathed

Underland in an orangey glimmer. The tall gas lamps which lit the streets hissed and added their own flickering yellow luminance, so that Underland felt as though it were in a state of permanent twilight. Beneath the smells of the city – horses and mouldering street food – the air smelled of wet earth and bonfires.

Malice had wondered if the portal might deliver them to her parents' Haunting Agency in the Haunting Quarter, but as she looked up at the building from which they'd just emerged, she saw it was an old flour mill and the noises coming from the streets beyond were the jovial sounds of the Underland Market. *Typical,* thought Malice; nothing in Underland was ever where you'd expect it to be.

Grandad saw her looking at the building.

"Munificence Malign owned a mill, back in the day," he replied to her unasked question. "So that she could grind her own flour to make bread for the poor."

"No wonder the other ancestors don't like her," said

Malice. "She really was a goody-two-shoes!"

Grandad laughed.

"What's it used for now?" Malice asked.

Grandad shrugged.

"No idea. I didn't even know the portal was still functioning."

The cobbled streets of the Underland Market were always bustling, but today the crowds of toffs, paupers and street-seller ghosts teemed thickly in a tide of top hats, flat caps and muddy petticoats.

"They're all going the same way," said Seth.

"Everyone's headed for the courthouse," Uncle Vex replied, pointing ahead to where the towers of an imposing gothic building loomed over crooked Tudor buildings and market stalls.

Rancid Roadkill and Tainted Loaf, the butchers' and bakers' stalls had "closed" signs hanging from their tent poles. But the Charcoal Chestnuts stall and the little cake shop on the corner – Putrid Patisserie –

were doing a roaring trade, as were the coffee shops, as ghosts grabbed snacks and drinks for the show about to start at the courthouse.

"It's been a long time since there was a crime as scandalous as Topunders ghostnapping an Underlander," said Grandad. "Looks like the whole Underland Market wants a piece of the action."

"Everyone, hold on to the person in front of you," warned Uncle Vex. "When we step off this pavement we'll be swept up in the melee and I don't want to lose any of you."

"Like you lost your apprentice that time in the sorcerers' parade?" asked Mayor Dawdle. "I remember it like it was yesterday – he was a lovely lad…"

"Yes, thank you, Mayor Dawdle, this is no time for a trip down nightmare lane." Uncle Vex cut the mayor off. "Everybody ready? One, two, three…"

They stepped into the throng. Uncle Vex held Malice's hand, who held Seth's, who held Grandad's, who held the mayor's; Antipathy-Rose clung to Grandad and snapped her sharp teeth at any ghouls who came too close. The tide of ghosts propelled them down dark narrow passages and along winding shop-lined streets. As they sailed on past a sweet shop called Mangy Molars, Seth called out, "Can we stop for some grim-gobstoppers?" He'd bought some during their last investigation: cabbage water and duckweed flavour.

"No time, I'm afraid, old boy," Uncle Vex called behind him. "Maybe on the way back."

Luckily for them, the ghosts' focus to reach the courthouse was so intense that nobody noticed Mayor Dawdle – still supposedly being held to ransom and the subject of all the excitement – marching along beside them.

The courthouse was made of black stone which sparkled in the streetlights and looked more than a little foreboding, especially with the flock of ravens circling its turrets in a cloud of dark feathers.

As the crowd spilled into the front courtyard of the building, a bell began to toll signalling that the hearing was about to begin. The crowd surged forward, causing a bottleneck at the front doors. There was no way to get through; they were stuck fast in a ghost-jam. At this rate, by the time they reached the entrance the hearing would be over.

"Quick!" said Uncle Vex, suddenly veering off

diagonally. "There's a side entrance. Follow me."

It wasn't easy running against the crowd, but soon they rounded a corner and found themselves alone in a dingy side alley. Uncle Vex stopped at an innocuous looking door.

He tapped on the door three times in quick succession, then twice slowly and then four times fast. At first there was no response and Malice wondered if they should get her sister to bite through the bars on one of the windows and climb in. But after a moment they were greeted by the sound of many locks squeaking and groaning as they were pulled back.

The door creaked open and a tiny old woman in a long skirt and shawl stood before them. She was puffing on a pipe and wore gold hoop earrings the size of saucers.

"Vexatious." She had a reedy voice. "I thought you'd be comin'," she said in a strong Bristolian accent. "'Oo you got with you then?"

Uncle Vex stepped back and introduced Malice and Seth and Antipathy-Rose.

The woman nodded at each of them in turn and then said, "All right, Grandad?"

"'Allo, Edna," Grandad replied. "Will you be giving another of your talks at the Grandads' Club soon? I really enjoyed your symposium on medieval weaponry last month."

Edna puffed on her pipe and raised an eyebrow.

"I might," she said enigmatically. "You'll be Tetchy-Sue's girl then," she went on, nodding towards Malice.

"Do you know her?" Malice asked.

"I went to Mischief Academy with your Nana Rascally. We stayed in touch after. I remember your ma when she was a girl; absolute troublemaker, I liked her a lot. Never thought she'd stoop to ghostnapping mind."

"She hasn't," said Malice. "We think she's been framed."

Edna gave a long slow blink in response and turned

her attention to Mayor Dawdle.

"You don't look very ghostnapped to me," she said slowly.

"Not any more, no," agreed the mayor.

"Well! You'd better get on in there then and see what's what."

The old woman stepped aside for them to go in.

"Wait!" she said, as Seth passed by her. She took three good puffs on her pipe and blew the murky smoke over Seth, who coughed as politely as possible. Then she wiped both her hands down the slimy stone wall and rubbed them over his cheeks before finally pulling a wodge of moss – at least Malice hoped it was moss – out of her pocket and wedged a clump behind each of his ears. Then she leaned in and sniffed him. "Better," she said. "The way that crowd is riled up, if he goes in there stinking like a freshly washed Topsider, he won't get far. There's plenty of Haunting Quarter ghosts have turned out for the spectacle, and if they

get a whiff of him, they'll eat him alive." She looked deep into Seth's eyes and said, "Literally alive!"

Seth gulped and said in a squeaky voice, "Thank you very much."

"Ah, yes. Good call," mused Uncle Vex rubbing his smooth chin. "Probably should have thought of that myself. Wouldn't do at all to have an apprentice devoured by a Haunting Quarter ghost."

"Wouldn't be the first time," the woman croaked and both Seth and Malice gave Uncle Vex an enquiring look.

"It was a long time ago. I don't like to talk about it," was his response.

The two friends raised their eyebrows at each other in unison.

Uncle Vex led them down a dark skinny corridor with wood panelling on one side. Malice could hear excitable chatter on the other side of it and assumed that must be the courtroom.

"Shouldn't *we* be in the courtroom?" Malice asked. "I understand why the mayor has to stay hidden, but we don't."

"I know this is hard for you, old girl," Uncle Vex said kindly. "Your instincts are to be out there supporting your parents. But right now, the biggest help you can be to Ma and Pa is to investigate on their behalf. One of the most important rules of detective work is observation. And we can observe best from back here where we have a perfect overview of the whole room, and any potential suspects won't be put on their guard by our presence."

Malice nodded. "I suppose you're right," she agreed. "Who was that woman who let us in?"

"That's Edna Cut-Throat, the courthouse security guard," Uncle Vex replied.

Seth sniggered. "Security guard? She's weeny, and she must be at least three hundred years old."

"Young man, have you not learned yet that looks can be deceiving? Edna Cut-Throat is feared throughout Underland. Mention her name in any tavern and it's an instant conversation stopper. If she doesn't want you in the courthouse, you aren't getting in."

Seth looked unconvinced.

"But she let you in," Malice commented.

"Oh, Edna and I go way back. She was my jiu-jitsu master."

Seth stifled another laugh but was spared a further lecture when Uncle Vex stopped abruptly and the rest of them banged into him, each squishing against the other like a concertina.

He motioned for them to be quiet and flicked his hands along the wooden wall, sliding open a series of small shutters. As each shutter snapped back, two holes appeared, spilling tubes of light into the corridor. Each set of holes were eye width apart.

Malice nodded as her understanding dawned.

"Peeping portraits," she whispered to Seth.

"Huh?" Seth replied.

"On the other side of this panelling there'll be a row of portraits, currently missing their eyes. We can watch the proceedings through the eyeholes."

"That is genius," Seth whispered back, awed. "I wonder if I could fix something like this up in my kitchen at home. I'm sure one or both of my dads keeps sneaking all the chocolate biscuits out of the tin."

They each took their place in front of a set of eyeholes.

Through hers, Malice surveyed the courtroom. Row upon row of chairs circled up from the ground like an amphitheatre, all of them filled with eager-faced ghosts. Those who hadn't managed to get a seat below had crowded into the gallery above where it was standing room only, ghosts and ghouls packed

in like sardines. She couldn't see her parents, but Vendetta and Animosity Grudge were sitting right near the front. Vendetta was wringing her hands while Animosity idly plaited his beard. Malice appreciated them being here – with Chief Braggart acting as though the case was already closed, her parents would need someone on their side, that was for sure.

GUILTY UNTIL
PROVEN INNOCENT

The noise in the stalls and the gallery above was rising to deafening, even from their position behind the wall. Then a ghost, who looked as though she'd been stretched on a rack, in a floor-length red robe and a long, dirty wig (Malice could see the lice crawling over it from where she peeped) entered the room. The Judge. The tumult instantly died down.

"Hello," Uncle Vex said quietly. "Where's Judge Staunch?"

"He's got the pox," Mayor Dawdle replied in a hushed voice. "This is his replacement, Judge Vulpine. She arrived at short notice from Terror Island – she comes highly recommended."

The judge climbed a set of steps to a throne shaped like a giant skull, its mouth dropped open in a silent scream. She settled herself on a red cushion inside the bottom half of the jaw and banged a hammer down on the desk in front of her.

"We are here to hear the case of the Ghosts of Underland against Topunders Pugnacious and Tetchy-Sue Malign in the matter of the ghostnapping of Mayor Tardy Dawdle. Would the accused please take the stand."

An usher brought out Ma and Pa, still in handcuffs, and walked them through the baying crowd.

Ma and Pa were holding hands around their handcuffs. They looked small and frightened in the dock, with the crowd shouting and booing at them.

Malice's heart squeezed. Her parents were such big characters – sure, they were stinky and dirty and had low moral standards, but they were still her parents and it broke Malice's heart to see them so diminished.

She had to help them, she just had to. She wanted to call out to them, to tell them that she loved them and believed them, but it would be better for everyone if she stayed quiet and watchful for now.

The judge addressed the court.

"For the benefit of the court, the information we have is that at some time in the night, between her last

appointment of the day and her first of the following day, the mayor of Underland, Ms Tardy Dawdle was ghostnapped. The authorities were alerted this morning when Ms Dawdle failed to show up for her 7 a.m. breakfast meeting. When police entered Ms Dawdle's apartment, they found signs of a struggle. A ransom note was subsequently delivered to the Underland Police Station. The hunt for the mayor continues. The accused refuse to cooperate."

The ghosts in the courtroom were captivated. The judge turned her cold gaze towards Ma and Pa.

"You stand accused of ghostnapping the mayor of Underland. How do you plead?"

Ma and Pa raised their chins defiantly.

"Not guilty!" they said.

The crowd roared its disapproval. Even the judge, who was supposed to be impartial, raised her eyebrows and tutted.

"For the benefit of the court, please tell us where

you were last night."

Pa cleared his throat. "I was on my mischief rounds, filling the fountain in the park with slime."

"And did anybody see you?"

"What kind of mischief-maker would I be if people saw me?"

Next it was Ma's turn to speak.

"I was stealing the pumpkins from the Felicity Square Garden's community allotment."

"Did anyone witness this mischief?" asked the judge.

"I do not make it my business to have my mischief witnessed!" said Ma defensively. Not being caught was a matter of pride for a mischief-maker. In this instance, though, Malice considered, their pride may see them heading for a fall.

"Can you explain to the court why your cutlass was found at the scene of the crime?"

At this, her parents' bravado suffered a puncture.

"No," they answered quietly.

The judge tented her fingers in front of her face.

"So, as it stands, *you* have no alibi for the night in question but *we* have evidence of you being at Mayor Dawdle's apartment in the form of your cutlass." She sneered smugly. "Are there any character witnesses for the accused?" the judge asked disinterestedly.

The Grudges tentatively raised their hands and Malice felt a surge of hope. They would tell the court that her parents were not ghostnappers and the judge would let them go home due to lack of evidence, and Malice could concentrate on tracking down the real culprits.

"Stand and give your testimony," ordered the judge.

The Grudges shuffled forward. "How long have you known the accused?" the judge demanded.

"Approximately forty-five years, Your Honour," answered Animosity.

"Have the accused been acting strangely lately?

More cagey than usual?" the judge continued.

"No, Your Worshipness, no more strange or cagey than normal," said Vendetta.

"In your opinion, would the accused want to get their mitts on the loot in the Underland Bank vaults?"

Animosity and Vendetta looked at one another nervously. *What kind of a question is that?* Malice wondered. It didn't seem very fair. Everyone knew that loot was her family's particular forte.

"Er, well, Your Judginess," Animosity began hesitatingly. "I mean, wouldn't any self-respecting Topunder want to get their hands on that kind of loot?"

"It doesn't mean they'd actually do it, though," added Vendetta.

"Answer the question," Judge Vulpine demanded. "Given the opportunity, would the Maligns steal the swag from the vaults?"

The Grudges looked pained but nodded their heads.

"Yes," they said.

The judge looked down at the papers in front of her and then back up at the Grudges.

"I understand that Pugnacious Malign is hoping to train his youngest daughter and her uncannily sharp gnashers to open safes in the future?" asked the judge.

Where was all this coming from? Malice thought. *How could she know that?* This didn't seem like a professional line of questioning at all. Weren't judges supposed to be impartial?

"Well, yes," said Animosity. "But I don't think he had the Underland Bank in mind…"

"Can you be sure?" boomed the judge. "Would you stake your life on it?"

Animosity loosened his collar.

"No, Your Honour," he answered quietly.

"Did you know that the Maligns have a private portal to Underland?" she asked.

A whisper went around the room at this.

"No, Your Magisterialness," said Vendetta.

"Would you describe the Maligns as secretive?"

Animosity sighed audibly and nodded his head.

"Yes," he said.

The judge looked annoyingly pleased with herself.

"Faced with the lack of any alibi at all for last night, their unashamed greed for loot and their sneaky nature, can you be one hundred per cent sure that the Maligns are innocent? Would you stake your son's life on it?"

"That's a low blow," whispered Uncle Vex.

"She does seem a little harsh," agreed Mayor Dawdle.

"Well!" Judge Vulpine thundered.

Animosity and Vendetta shrugged in apology at Ma and Pa, who stood with sagging shoulders in the dock.

"No," said the Grudges.

"Speak up!" the judge demanded.

"No, Your Honour, we can't be sure the Maligns

are innocent."

A fox-like grin played across Judge Vulpine's mouth.

"Mayor Dawdle remains missing, despite our best efforts to find her. It is my view that the Maligns are a danger to society…"

Malice's mind was reeling. This couldn't be happening! Before she knew what she was doing, she found herself banging on the panelled walls.

"Wait!" she yelled, kicking and punching at the wall which just wouldn't budge. "Wait! I have new evidence."

THE SPEED AND FEROCITY
OF A DERANGED BEAVER

"What are you doing, old girl?" asked Uncle Vex
in alarm.

"We have to show them that the mayor is safe. We
have to let her give her testimony now!" said Malice
breathlessly.

By now Seth and the mayor had joined in trying
to break the wall down. Antipathy-Rose wriggled out
of Grandad's arms and toddled over to Malice. She
tugged on Malice's pinafore and pointed to her teeth.

"Good idea, Anti," said Malice. "Go for it!"

Antipathy-Rose pressed her face to the panelling and began gnawing at the wood with the speed and ferocity of a deranged beaver. Sawdust flew in all directions. In no time at all, she had sawn a hole big enough for them to climb through.

One by one, to the shocked awe of the ghosts and Ma and Pa, they emerged into the courtroom and dusted themselves down. A unified gasp went up when the mayor stepped into view.

Judge Vulpine had paled with rage.

"What is the meaning of this?" she roared.

Malice almost lost her nerve, but the pride on her parents' faces gave her courage.

"Your Honour," Malice stepped forward. "We have found Mayor Dawdle and, as you can see, she is unharmed. My parents are innocent. They've been framed for a crime they didn't commit."

The courtroom was in uproar, but a sharp wrap of

the judge's gavel on her desk brought the noise down to a loud whisper.

"Ms Dawdle, now that you are here, perhaps you could furnish us with the details of your harrowing ghostnap."

The mayor, whose glasses constantly slipped down her nose, pushed them back up again and began to tell her sorry tale. Her floral neck scarf drifted out behind her, as though in preparation for her to begin running at any moment.

"Well, I was in my office, finishing up for the day," she began.

"And what time was this?" interrupted the judge.

"7 p.m., Your Honour."

"Are you sure?"

"Yes, Your Honour. My grandfather clock had just chimed the hour."

The judge nodded and the mayor continued.

"All of sudden, someone came up behind me and

put a sack over my head and bundled me off. At first, I thought it was a prank, you know, what with me being new to the job and all. But after they'd thrown me into an oubliette and left me, I realized it probably wasn't a joke."

"And were you able to ascertain any distinguishing features about your ghostnappers?" asked Judge Vulpine.

Mayor Dawdle pushed her glasses up her nose again and nodded.

"The one who grabbed me was female, I think. I could hear her jewellery jangling and she said, 'I've got 'er, Pa. Grab 'er legs.'"

Malice's heart began to sink.

"Then the other one said, 'good one, my ferret-faced fart bag.'"

Holy Gravediggers! thought Malice. *That's just the kind of thing Pa would say to Ma.* Whoever had framed her parents knew them well enough to copy

their mannerisms.

"Anything else?" asked the judge.

"They smelled musty. Even with the bag over my head I could smell them; a bit like greasy dog."

"That does sound like your Pa," Seth whispered, and Malice nodded grimly.

"Thank you, Mayor Dawdle," the judge smiled unpleasantly. "You have been most helpful. But this changes nothing."

"B-but," the mayor stuttered. "I haven't identified the Maligns. I couldn't even if I wanted to because I have no idea who ghostnapped me!"

"You are dismissed." The judge waved the mayor away lazily. "Just one more question before you go," she added. "Where were you being held?"

Mayor Dawdle hesitated. She looked at the judge and then Ma and Pa and then at Malice, with an apology in her eyes, and Malice's heart sank.

"I was in the oubliette at Malignant House," said

the mayor in a small voice.

Sounds of collective dismay whooshed around the courtroom. Judge Vulpine's eyes lit up like an owl who's just spotted a tasty mouse. She licked her lips and addressed Ma and Pa.

"The mayor was discovered in your oubliette. The Malign family have a rich and infamous history in pilfering and plundering loot. I see no alternative but to find you guilty until proven innocent. This court will adjourn for twenty-four hours to allow for fact finding. If, after that time, there is no evidence to support your claim of innocence, you will be sentenced to live out your days in the Underland Crypts, where you will only be permitted to see your family once every ten years."

"No!" Malice cried out. Her cry was loud in the suddenly silent courtroom. The same shock that Malice felt was expressed on the faces of the ghosts in the amphitheatre and galleries. Even the police looked

taken aback. Judge Vulpine's threatened sentence seemed like a cruel and unusual punishment.

Only the judge herself seemed unmoved.

"Take them away!" she demanded.

The ushers pulled Malice's parents from the dock to lead them back to the dungeons.

"We've been wronged!" shouted Ma. "And our daughter, Malice Morbid Malign, will prove it!"

"Because she is the cleverest, bravest Malign there's ever been!" added Pa, and Ma nodded vigorously.

"We believe in you!" Ma's voice echoed around the courtroom as she and Pa were swept out of sight and a heavy door banged shut behind them.

Malice felt the tears running down her cheeks. She had always felt like a disappointment to her parents, what with her bathing and reading, but she saw now that wasn't true at all; she was *different* to them, not disappointing. Uncle Vex pulled a silk, spotted handkerchief from his pocket and passed it to Malice.

"Come on, old girl," he said kindly. "Manifest those tears into salty globules of determination."

Seth gave her a hug.

"We've got this, Malice," he said. "We'll prove their innocence."

"Without a doubt!" Uncle Vex agreed.

"If there is anything at all I can do, don't hesitate to ask," said Mayor Dawdle. "But if you don't mind, I'd like to go home now. I feel in need of a long mud bath and a large glass of hemlock wine."

"You go, Tardy. Thank you for trying to help," said Grandad, shaking her hand vigorously.

"I only wish I could have done more," the mayor lamented. "I must admit, I had my doubts

at first. I don't mean to be rude, but I wouldn't have put something as devious as ghostnapping past Pugnacious and Tetchy-Sue. They have a fairly despicable reputation. And being thrust into their oubliette didn't exactly go in their favour. But your trust in their innocence is so strong that I find it hard to dispute. I may not have much faith in the accused themselves, but I believe in all of you, and that's proof enough for me."

"Thank you," said Malice. "That's very kind of you."

"You know where to find me." Mayor Dawdle smiled and laid a cold kiss on Malice's cheek before walking away.

The ghosts were clearing out of the courtroom in a much more orderly fashion than they had entered. Mayor Dawdle joined them.

"I'm a bit pooped, ducky," said Grandad. "I might pop to the Grandads' Club for a cup of tea and a little rest, if you don't mind?"

"Of course, Grandad." Malice hugged him tight.

"I'll keep my ear to the ground while I'm there. There's always plenty of gossip at the club. Would you like me to take Antipathy-Rose? She'll be no bother."

Malice looked down at her sister, who was clinging desperately on to her left leg like a koala to a tree trunk.

"No, thank you, Grandad, I'll keep Anti with me, I think."

Grandad nodded and kissed the top of her head.

"You are brave and kind and clever, duck," said Grandad. "If anyone can get to the bottom of this mess, you can."

Malice smiled, even though her mouth didn't feel like it, and watched as Grandad too joined the crowd leaving the courtroom.

A CLOCKWORK ESCALATOR

"Right," said Uncle Vex decisively. "We will need to approach this case methodically. Malice, how should we begin?"

Since Malice and Seth were Uncle Vex's official apprentices, he liked to test them on investigating procedures. Malice was grateful – she needed to be busy and to have her thoughts consumed by something other than sadness and worry.

"We need to search for clues," Malice began. "We need to start by gathering evidence in Ma's office,

looking for anything that doesn't belong to Ma or looks suspicious, or signs of an imposter having been there."

"Excellent!" said Uncle Vex. "Seth, what are our tools of the trade?"

Seth rifled through his pockets and pulled out several objects.

"Evidence envelopes, tweezers, magnifying glass, gloves and pen and paper," Seth replied proudly.

"Superb! Both of you. If you can work this well under pressure, you will make fine investigators. I suggest we take the Malign portal back to Malignant House since that is the criminal's most likely point of entry."

The way back up through the portal was less high-octane than the way down but no less of an experience.

The soldier guarding the portal woke grudgingly for just long enough to instruct them how to get back up to Topside and to record one of their names in his logbook, before he fell back to sleep.

"A clockwork escalator!" Uncle Vex exclaimed. "A remarkable feat of engineering. Before this, they used to employ ferrets to run round and round on a wheel to turn the cogs. But you know what ferrets are like: they're a feisty breed – kept going on strike to demand more pay."

Seth frowned as Uncle Vex took hold of a handle attached to a large, cogged wheel and began to turn it, puffing and straining as he did so.

"What did they pay the ferrets with?" he asked.

"Rats, mostly. London was lousy with them before they built the sewage systems; Topunders used to bring them down by the barrel load."

They were standing behind the helter-skelter, snow beneath their feet, snowflakes drifting gently skyward, tickling beneath their chins as they floated up. Before them was a wooden escalator reaching up into the swirling snow clouds above; the top was completely obscured. A wall of cogs, large and small, covered the side of the structure. And at the bottom of this wall, Uncle Vex wound the lowest cog, faster and faster, his quiff flopping up and down like a duck diving for pond bugs, his tall, thin frame bent over like a snapped bamboo timber with pointy shoes on.

After an awful lot of grunting and some inventive

swear words, Uncle Vex straightened up. The lowest cog was now turning under its own propulsion. The next cog caught in its craw, and it too began to turn. This continued slowly up the whole wall until every cog was turning and the air was filled with a sound like many ticking clocks. The escalator juddered into life and began to move.

"Hop on," said Uncle Vex, mopping his brow with his handkerchief.

Seth stepped on first. The wooden steps creaked and groaned. Malice swung her sister up on to her hip and went next, followed by Uncle Vex.

The escalator moved sedately and despite Malice's agitation to get on with the case, she couldn't help but be soothed as they passed through thick white clouds puffing out snow like one of Ma's powder puffs. Antipathy-Rose was lulled to sleep by the escalator's motion and as she nestled her hot little head into Malice's neck, Malice found she could think clearly

for the first time since that morning.

She felt bolstered by her parents' confidence in her and supported by Grandad, Seth and Uncle Vex. She needed to start thinking about her strengths rather than her weaknesses; it was all too easy to become despondent. She could speak to the night creatures; she was especially good at moth-whispering. She had a mind for working out puzzles and a keen eye for clues. And her witch ancestry helped her to think in a wily way – surely handy when trying to track down a villain intent on framing her parents. In many ways, the ghostnapper was just a glorified bully and Malice had lots of experience of bullies. *Yes!* she said to herself. *You can do this, Malice Morbid Malign.*

GOOD OLD-FASHIONED
INVISIBLE INK

Seth looked around Ma's dingy office.

"It's not the most inspiring place to work," he said,
surveying the windowless room.

"This is Topunder chic," said Malice. "Ma based it
on a picture she saw in her *Haunted Living* magazine.
She gets a lot of home design ideas from magazines."

"She did this on purpose?" Seth was sceptical.

Malice pulled out a filing cabinet drawer and laid
Antipathy-Rose down in it so she could finish her

nap. Her sister's sharp little gnashers meant that traditional dummies were quite useless at soothing her but brass doorknobs, the kind you might find on a chest of drawers, worked a treat. Malice popped the doorknob into Antipathy-Rose's mouth and the toddler sighed dreamily and went back to sleep.

Uncle Vex crouched down by the oubliette trapdoor with his magnifying glass. Seth searched the shelves for any signs of disturbance in the thick layers of dust which might offer some clues. Malice studied the floor near the cupboard doors where she had deduced the ghostnappers would have entered and left so as not to be seen by anyone in the house.

It wasn't easy to spot clues in amongst the bunny-sized dust bunnies but Malice noticed some gingery hairs trapped beneath one of the doors which definitely didn't belong to Ma. She tweezered them into one of her evidence envelopes and then crawled along the path the villains would most likely have

taken. **N**o footprints, worse luck, but she did find some chipped paint flecks which weren't in the colours of any of the many flaking doors and walls in Malignant House. Malice took out a fresh envelope and tipped them in before moving across to Ma's desk.

"Hold the torch for me would you, old boy?" Uncle Vex called across to Seth.

Seth trained the beam of light on the bottom of the oubliette, while Uncle Vex lowered an iron hook on the end of a rope down into the hole. After some mild cursing, Uncle Vex reeled the rope back up. Hanging from the hook was a hessian sack.

"Is that the bag used to cover the mayor's head?" Malice asked, looking up from an open box file.

"I think we can assume so, yes."

With his free hand, Uncle Vex fished around in his pocket and pulled out a large paper bag which he handed to Seth.

"Hold that open would you, old chap?" he asked,

163

and dropped the sack into it. "You never know, there could be evidence on it. Pop it in your rucksack, Seth. If I stuff that in my pocket it'll rumple my suit."

Malice was sifting methodically through the chaos on Ma's desk. She had opened one of the drawers beneath the desk but upon finding a warrant for Pa's arrest dated 1963, she had decided to leave the drawers alone.

Most of the paperwork pertained to the Haunting Agency and the preparations for the All Hallows' Haunt, so Malice set about separating them into subject piles. Ma really had worked hard to make the Haunt a success. There were lists of buffet foods and recipes, some with little added sidenotes like: *glazed beetles are Vex's favourite* or *add extra cheese mould to fungal fancies for Nana Rascally.* And Ma had commissioned a thousand candles to be made using her own stink bomb scent, to create just the right ambience. Along the far wall, floor to ceiling

shelves were lined with demijohns filled with a dark orange liquid which glooped and bubbled: Ma's homemade pumpkin wine, guaranteed to dissolve tonsils and strip paint.

To Malice's mind, this was evidence enough that her parents had nothing to do with the mayor's ghostnap; why would they risk all their hard work by ghostnapping the very woman who was due to declare the All Hallows' Haunt open on the big night? Answer: they wouldn't. But she would need more than a few lists and some caustic wine to prove it to the authorities. She needed cold hard evidence.

While Seth and Uncle Vex continued to comb the area around the oubliette, Malice put together a list of the acquaintances most likely to want to frame Ma and Pa. It had been hard to whittle it down. But they needed to shine their focus somewhere and they might as well begin by eliminating the most obvious suspects.

1. Mordacious and Truculent MacNe'erdoowell

   Why? Because they made no secret of their annoyance at being passed over as hosts for the All Hallows' Haunt. And with Ma and Pa incapacitated, the hosting has been passed back to them.

2. Any of the four Topunder families snubbed by Ma and Pa

   Names:
   - The Shropshire Pinchers
   - The Essex Racketeers
   - The Newcastle Brigands
   - The Bristol Savages

3. Most of Underland

   Why? Because my parents have a way of really annoying everyone.

"Gracious!" said Uncle Vex, looking over the list. "Having to glean alibis from The MacNe'erdoowells, Pinchers, Racketeers, Brigands and the Savages ought to keep us busy for a while."

"Are they all Topunders?" Seth asked.

"Yes," Malice replied. "There are quite a few ghosts who aren't keen on my parents, but they wouldn't be solid by the time they reached Topside, so they wouldn't have been able to lift the oubliette trapdoor."

"That, my dear niece, is called thinking out of the coffin! Good deducing."

Antipathy-Rose snuffled and woke up growling. She was always cranky when she woke from her nap and Malice dug around in her pinafore pocket for something for her to chew. She pulled out a turkey leg bone and as she did so the piece of paper she'd found earlier fell out.

"What's this?" asked Seth, picking it up and turning it over in his hands.

"Oh, just something I caught Anti trying to throw in the fire earlier."

"There's nothing on it," said Seth.

"Well, that's the weird thing," agreed Malice, bouncing her sister on her knee. "I grabbed it because I could have sworn I saw writing on it, but when I looked at it again, it was blank."

Uncle Vex twirled his quiff.

"Near the fire, you say?"

"Yes. It was probably just my imagination." Malice felt suddenly silly. They had far bigger things to worry about than some disappearing words on a scrap of paper.

Uncle Vex took the paper from Seth and turned it over in his hand.

"Nothing there now," he said to himself. "Unless … the heat…"

Malice watched as her uncle pulled a handkerchief from his pocket and used it to protect his hand from

the heat as he unscrewed the glass shade of one of the gas lamps. He then carefully flattened the note around the hot shade.

Seth and Malice drew near to watch. As if by magic, a list of squiggles began to appear on the previously blank page.

"Woah!" said Seth. "Magic paper!"

"Nothing so exciting, old boy. This is merely good old-fashioned invisible ink. Heat activated."

The squiggles became clear, and Malice drew in a sharp intake of breath as she saw it was numbers, brackets and letters, none of which made any sense to her:

$$(8,7)$$
$$D: 40xF$$

"What does it mean?" asked Malice.

"I don't know." Uncle Vex rubbed his chin.

"Do you recognize the writing?" asked Seth.

Malice shrugged.

"It's hard to tell with so little to go on. It could be Pa's, but it could just as easily be something Pa swiped when he was out on his mischief rounds. Then again, the house is so full at the moment with the preparations for the Haunt that anyone could have dropped it."

"Do you think it's a clue? Or another mystery waiting to be solved?" asked Seth.

Uncle Vex chewed the inside of his cheek.

"I don't want to rule it out as it's obviously important; people don't just write in invisible ink for fun … unless they're me. I'm just not sure how or if it pertains to this particular case. Either way, it was a good spot, Malice. Well done. Keep it safe."

Malice folded the paper up neatly and pushed it between the pages of her notebook for safekeeping.

"I think we've gathered just about all the evidence

we can from this room," said Uncle Vex, taking a lint roller out of his suit pocket and rollering himself all over; Uncle Vex did not like fluff on his sharp suit. "Now, may I suggest we regroup and build up our strength by paying a visit to the Vengeful Brew? I think some of Belladonna's devil's foot cake is just the ticket! And I don't like to leave too big a gap between tea breaks. It's a bad habit to get into."

"Did you say devil's *foot* cake?" Seth asked.

"Yes," said Uncle Vex.

"Fair enough, then." Seth nodded.

PURVEYOR OF POTENTIALLY POISONOUS PATISSERIES

They decided to take the lift in the old oak tree down to Underland as Charon, the lift operator, could deliver you directly to pretty much anywhere you wanted to go. As they walked through Felicity Square, they experienced the usual curtain twitching from the terribly snobby residents. Malice always kept her head down as she walked; she didn't like being the subject of their scorn. But Uncle Vex raised his panama hat to each and every curtain-twitcher,

calling, "Top of the morning to you!" and bestowing upon them his most charming smile. Antipathy-Rose bit chunks out of the bone she was gnawing and spat it at their windows. She was a surprisingly good shot – the crack of bone on glass echoed around the quiet square. Seth sniggered, "Good one, Anti!" and Antipathy-Rose's cheeks glowed with pleasure.

Charon was waiting for them, the buttons on his bellboy uniform glinting in the sun. He had quite the friendliest face on a skeleton Malice had ever seen … and she had seen a lot of skeletons.

"Greetings, Miss Malice, Mr Vexatious, Master Seth and Miss Antipathy-Rose. Where can I take you on this fine day?"

"Hello, Charon," said Malice, smiling. "We'd like to go to the Vengeful Brew please."

"Afternoon teatime, is it?" asked Charon, as he ushered them into the small lift.

"One doesn't like to miss it if one can help it,"

Uncle Vex replied.

Seth didn't say anything. The whole chatting with skeletons and hanging around in Underland with the undead was still quite new to him and he hadn't quite got past being struck dumb with awed admiration. Malice loved how much he enjoyed it all; it was wonderful to have a friend to share her bizarre life with. Most people would have run a mile as soon as they found out Malice lived in a house full of ghosts. But not Seth.

Charon ran a bony finger along a display of hundreds of glowing buttons while the others strapped themselves in. Uncle Vex had pulled a silk scarf over his hat and tied it under his chin.

"There we are," said Charon, finding the right button. "The Vengeful Brew. Everybody ready?"

They all nodded their consent, the lift music began – Vivaldi today – and they plunged downwards. The interesting thing about the old oak tree lift was that

as you plummeted at speed, you were also being dragged left, right, horizontal and diagonal; it was very confusing for the internal organs and hair.

The lift came to a stop and Malice waited for her kidneys to settle back to their rightful positions before undoing her harness.

"Please step on to the exit," said Charon, and they took their places on a square marked out on the floor of the lift. Charon pushed a button and the floor opened up beneath their feet and they all tumbled down and landed in a tangled heap on a pile of cushions.

The portal entrance to the Vengeful Brew was a broom cupboard, but since Malice visited so often, Belladonna, the tearoom's glamorous owner, had covered the floor with cushions for a softer landing.

The Vengeful Brew was situated in the heart of the Haunting Quarter. The tearoom was what you might call *noir chic*, from the black lace tablecloths

to the chandeliers above which dripped
with black crystals, to the black
painted walls. Its clientele
ranged from the mischievous to
the downright naughty and every ghost in between.
Belladonna had recently branched out into chocolate
making and her Cursed Confectionary range was
pulling in the dead from far and wide.

The place was packed, and they only got seats
because a table of witches were gathering up their
broomsticks to leave as they walked in. The table
was close to the fire, slightly away from the main
hubbub, and Seth and Malice warmed their hands
gratefully, while Uncle Vex twirled his quiff and
straightened his tie.

"Greetings, confidantes," Belladonna purred in
her French accent. She had glided up so quietly they
hadn't seen her coming. As usual, she was wearing
an exquisite floor-length ball gown of crushed black

silk. Her features were sharp like her wit and Malice liked her enormously.

"Hi, Belladonna," said Malice and Seth together.

Uncle Vex, who always flushed when he saw Belladonna, fiddled with his pocket watch. Belladonna – who in Malice's opinion had grown tired of waiting for Uncle Vex to ask her out – had been dating a ghoul in the Wild Witch Woods for a while, but in the end the distance between them had

proved too much. Uncle Vex had a certain spring in his step ever since he'd heard the news. Malice wondered if her uncle would ever stop beating around the funeral pyre and ask the beautiful purveyor of potentially poisonous patisseries out on a date.

"Ah, Belladonna, you are looking strange and unusual as always," said Uncle Vex, trying and failing to look casual.

Belladonna nodded in satisfaction at the compliment.

"Thank you, Vex. I am sorry to hear about your parents, Malice," she said. "Are they guilty?"

"No," said Malice, not at all offended by Belladonna's directness; it was one of the many things she liked about her. "Not this time."

Belladonna nodded once to indicate that she believed her.

"You're on the Underland Council, aren't you?" asked Malice.

179

"I am the Haunting Quarter representative," Belladonna confirmed.

"Were you at the breakfast meeting this morning?"

"I was. Of course, it had to be abandoned when the mayor didn't show up."

"Who raised the alarm?"

"Animosity Grudge. Tardy Dawdle is well known for her lateness, but she always arrives eventually. When she didn't, Animosity arranged for the mayor's secretary to visit her house. He would have gone himself, but he had somewhere else to be – your house, I believe."

"What were the Grudges doing at an Underland Council meeting?" asked Malice.

"They were requesting planning permission, or was it demolition permission? I can't recall which, I was too perturbed by the way Vendetta's abominable coat kept moulting over my ball gown. I offered to burn it for her, but she declined. She ought to be arrested for crimes against style."

Uncle Vex smirked smugly in the way of one supremely confident in his sense of style.

"So, they left before the mayor's ghostnap was discovered?" asked Seth.

"Correct. Malice, your sister is eating my crockery," Belladonna raised one sculpted eyebrow.

"Oh, gurgling gargoyles!" Malice exclaimed glancing down at Antipathy-Rose. Little piles of dust and shards of floral china were collecting on the table

as her sister gnawed her way through her second teacup. "Sorry, Belladonna. I'll pay for the damage."

Belladonna waved a dismissive hand and smiled benignly.

"Don't give it another thought. She reminds me of my sister, Strychnine, when she was a baby. Always devouring someone; a little tyke she was. I've got some rock cakes just out of the oven – I'll bring her some over. I only use the finest rocks sourced from the Carpathian Mountains."

"Thank you," said Malice, pushing the rest of the crockery out of reach.

"I say, old girl," began Uncle Vex. "You're a woman who keeps her ear to the ground. You haven't noticed anything fishy going on, have you? This case is proving tough to crack."

"There have been a lot of suspicious goings on recently," said Belladonna quietly. "It can be hard to see the bones for the flesh."

"Aren't all the goings on in Underland suspicious?" Seth asked.

Belladonna smiled indulgently at him.

"*Touché*, Topunder. It is a question of observance. I watch and I listen. In a world where the extraordinary is ordinary, you must look closely to find the anomalies."

"Can you tell us some of the suspicious goings on?" asked Malice.

Antipathy-Rose had wiggled herself off Malice's lap and toddled away around the tearoom.

"Cast your eyes covertly to the table in the far corner by the cake-coffin and tell me what you see," said Belladonna.

The three investigators did their best impression of seeming not to look at the table in the corner. Two women and two men sat scowling at each other, their heads pulled in close. Clearly, they didn't want anyone to hear their discussion.

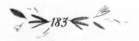

LIKE A PORK CHOP AT A
VEGAN CONVENTION

"They look familiar," said Malice. "They're Topunders, aren't they?"

"Not just any Topunders," Uncle Vex confirmed. "What you have there is the heads of four of the most infamous Topunder families in the UK. The woman with the hair like lank seaweed is known as Stinky Pincher, and opposite her, the man with two green snot trails, is Phlegm Brigand."

"That's right!" said Malice. "Now I know where

I've seen them – they were at the MacNe'erdoowell's ball last year."

"The woman licking the curdled cream off all the toxic eclairs and putting them back in the cake-coffin is a frequent visitor to the Haunting Quarter – her name is Po-Face Savage. And the man next to her is Gaseous Racketeer," added Belladonna.

"Those are the four families not invited to the Halloween Ball!" exclaimed Malice. "They're on my list! Why would they be here all together?"

"That is very suspicious!" said Seth.

"Yes!" Belladonna smiled indulgently at Seth. "You see, in a room full to the brim with suspicious activities, that one stands out from the rest."

"It could be a revenge thing," said Malice, suddenly excited. "They might have framed my parents for not inviting them to the ball."

"Seems a bit petty," said Seth.

"You've met my parents, right?" Malice

replied wryly.

"No slight is too small to avenge when it comes to Topunders," said Uncle Vex.

"We need to hear what they're saying." Malice's mind was whirring.

"I'll go over; I'm good at looking unassuming," said Seth helpfully, getting up from his seat.

Uncle Vex put a hand on his arm to stop him.

"I hate to break it to you, old boy, but down in Underland there is *nothing* unassuming about you. You stick out like a pork chop at a vegan convention."

Seth looked around the tearoom; at least one pair of eyes from each table was cast in his direction, and none of them looked friendly. He gulped and shuffled back down into his chair.

"Don't worry, Seth. No one will bother you whilst you are under my roof," Belladonna soothed.

"What about when I'm not under your roof?"

She shrugged and said vaguely, "I'm sure your

lanyard will act as a deterrent against the worst of the hexes."

"I'll go," said Malice. "Watch Anti for me."

And before anyone could object, she jumped up and headed over to the cake-coffin where she pretended to be choosing a patisserie. The Topunders at the table didn't even notice her.

"I think we should call it off," whispered Stinky Pincher, and Po-Face nodded in agreement.

"And what if they get out?" growled Gaseous. "I've put in too much effort to see it all go to waste."

Malice's heart was in her mouth. There was no way they weren't talking about her parents. She focused hard on a curdled-cream spinach eclair and listened.

"We've all put in the hours to make our scheme work, but the evidence against them is pretty damning. I'd be surprised if they get out of this," said Phlegm, rubbing his hands with glee.

"They've had it coming," sneered Po-Face. "Who do

they think they are not inviting us to the All Hallows' Haunt? I'll admit it would be a shame after all our efforts not to be able to see the look on their faces. But the charges against them are an absolute gift."

Malice tried to slow her breathing down. This was as good as a confession.

"Banged up, and we didn't have to lift a finger," Stinky sniggered and the others joined in.

"The mischief gods have certainly been smiling on us," added Gaseous.

Malice had heard enough. She weaved her way back through the tables to where Uncle Vex and Seth were tucking into wodges of cake.

"I wouldn't have thought it could work when you first said it," Seth was saying. "But the pond slime really gives the frosting a velvety finish."

"We really should research your family tree, Seth. I feel sure there must be some Topunder in you somewhere," replied Uncle Vex.

"It was them," Malice blurted, shovelling in a forkful of cake. "They practically confessed it."

One of Uncle Vex's eyebrows arched enquiringly.

"Well, I must say, that was easier than I'd expected. Let's finish our tea and decide how to confront them."

"Where's Anti?" Malice asked, looking around.

A yelping sound came from by the window. They looked over and saw a pirate holding his wooden leg above his head as Antipathy-Rose stood on his lap, reaching her little arms up towards it.

"Oh no!" Malice exclaimed.

"Sorry, old girl. Only took our eyes off her for a second."

"It's the frosting on this cake," said Seth. "It's all-consuming."

Malice extracted Antipathy-Rose from the pirate, by which time she had climbed up his face and was standing on his head still reaching for his leg.

"So sorry," said Malice, as her sister reached her

190

arms out to the pirate and snapped her jaws.

"Arrhhhhgggh!" the pirate replied. "She's only doing what comes natural to her. Bring her to me when she's grown and she can have a job on my ghost ship. Always good to have someone like her on the crew for treasure hunting."

Antipathy-Rose grinned unexpectedly and clapped her hands. Apparently she liked the idea.

Malice took her sister back to the table but only managed one slurp of Thames Sludge tea before the Topunders on her suspects list stood and sloped out of the tearoom.

"We need to follow them!" said Malice, jumping up and shoving several rock cakes into her pockets.

Seth quickly wrapped their cakes in napkins and stashed them in his rucksack. Uncle Vex sighed exaggeratedly.

"You know there used to be a time when everything stopped for afternoon tea; it was a respected tradition. Even villains ceased their villainy long enough to enjoy a scone and a brew. These days, nothing is sacred."

Malice rolled her eyes as she and Seth followed the Topunders out into the darkening afternoon, with Uncle Vex still grumbling about modernity and the lost art of taking tea behind them. The glow-worms in the earthen sky above were losing their battle against a cold blanket of fog which was unfurling itself across the land and the Haunting Quarter looked even more ominous than usual.

WE'RE MISCHIEF-MAKERS, NOT MONSTERS

They followed the suspects from the quiet streets of the Haunting Quarter to the contrastingly overcrowded area around Shifty Row, deftly avoiding the piles of horse manure which made the already slippery cobbles even more hazardous. As carriage wheels bounced through puddles, the three investigators jumped clear of the muck which splattered everything in its path. Naturally, Antipathy-Rose wanted to get down and paddle in

the sludge, but Malice kept a firm hold of her. She would find some manure for her to roll in later as a treat.

Ghostly gentlemen in top hats walked arm in arm with ladies whose long petticoats trailed in the mud, and flat-capped children danced between them playing stick and hoop.

Finally, the Topunders stopped and entered the Harridan Hotel, a building so old it was bent almost double. Malice, Seth and Uncle Vex followed them in.

"Now what?" hissed Seth as they entered the cramped and crooked entrance hall. "Do we just confront them?"

"I can't see them? Where did they go?" hissed Malice.

"Um, I think I've found them," squeaked Uncle Vex.

They turned and saw that Stinky Pincher had Uncle Vex in a headlock. She was flanked by the other three, who regarded them with varying expressions of hostility.

"Now, why don't we get comfortable in the Harridan's drawing room and have a nice, uncivilized chat," suggested Po-Face Savage, holding a mace in one hand and slapping it into the palm of the other.

Malice and Seth allowed themselves to be ushered into the drawing room, with Uncle Vex shuffling along behind, his head still firmly wedged in Stinky's armpit. Phlegm Brigand motioned for them to sit, and they did so, sinking into the chintzy sofa, upholstered in a fabric of rotting leaves and dead birds. Stinky finally released Uncle Vex and he collapsed down next to Malice.

"I will have to wash my hair at least ten times tonight, to get the stench out," he complained in a low voice as he did his best to restore his hair into some semblance of style.

Antipathy-Rose patted his knee reassuringly and spat a Carpathian Mountain rock at Stinky, who yelped and clasped her shoulder.

"Keep 'er under control, would ya!" Stinky complained.

Malice only smiled and hugged her sister tighter.

"Well done, Anti," she whispered. "Nobody puts our uncle in a headlock and gets away with it." Antipathy-Rose gurgled something unintelligible and snuggled in for a nap.

"Now then." Gaseous Racketeer twiddled a hatchet like a baton as he spoke. "Why are you following us around?"

"Ah, well now," Uncle Vex began haltingly. "Let me take a moment to explain, if I may. I'll get straight

to the point, best to avoid dilly-dallying in these situations, it's like this you see…"

"We believe my parents were framed for a crime they didn't commit, and we think you might have done it," Malice butted in. She felt her uncle and her friend stiffen by her side. Perhaps being direct wasn't the way to go after all.

The atmosphere in the room changed. Malice could hear Seth's nose whistling as his breathing became quicker.

"I can't believe it," said Stinky – she seemed to be deflating where she stood.

"Why, of all the hurtful…" began Gaseous, the hatchet hanging loosely at his side.

Po-Face's bottom lip quivered, and she looked away to hide her tears. Phlegm put a comforting arm around her shoulders.

"We've got feelings you know!" he said.

This was unexpected. Malice had been prepared

for aggression, an argument at the very least, but this?

"Er, sorry?" Malice offered.

"It just isn't fair to judge us by the way we look." Po-Face had finally found her voice.

"I didn't," said Malice quickly. "It wasn't anything to do with your looks."

"Not because my eyes are too close together?" asked Phlegm.

"Or because my hair's greasy?" asked Stinky.

"Or because my eyebrows resemble a draught excluder?" Gaseous sniffed.

"No!" Malice assured them. "None of those things. I thought perhaps you might have wanted to get back at them for not inviting you to the All Hallows' Haunt. And then when I heard you talking at the Vengeful Brew, it seemed to confirm my suspicions."

"We did want to get back at them, but not by sending them to jail," gasped Stinky.

"We're mischief-makers, not monsters!" added Po-Face.

"Then, what were you going to do?" asked Seth.

"We were gonna crash the Haunt, weren't we?" said Gaseous. "Bringing our whole families, we were, ancestors 'n' all; they're all back at the Weary Necromancer waiting for us to give them the go ahead."

"We figured if we turned up all together they couldn't turn us away. Teach 'em a lesson for excluding us," added Stinky. "Then we were gonna scoff every last canapé and glug every drop of mead. It was gonna be a sweet and tasty revenge."

"So, am I understanding this correctly, none of you had anything to do with Mayor Dawdle's ghostnap?" Malice asked. "And your big plan was to gatecrash the All Hallows' Haunt?"

"That is correct," said Phlegm.

"Ghostnapping's not our style," added Po-Face.

"Just for my records," Malice ventured. "Can you tell me where you were at seven o'clock last night?"

"Having dinner with your Nana Rascally," said Stinky. "Ask her if you like."

"And afterwards she took us out bat watching with her in the Wild Witch Woods," Po-Face added.

"There's been some sightings recently of the Red-eyed Reaper Bat," said Phlegm. "Very rare. We were lucky to spot it."

"Great Gallows!" exclaimed Uncle Vex. "You actually saw a Red-eyed Reaper?"

The four Topunders nodded.

"Do you know, that's been on my list of bats to spot for years. I can hardly believe it. I'll have to get down there myself." Uncle Vex was off on a tangent.

"It's worth doing," Po-Face encouraged.

"Oh, yes, it's a spectacle – you won't want to miss it," added Stinky.

While the others were engrossed in bat talk,

Malice used the Harridan Hotel's computer to send her Nana a ghoulagram. She wanted to double-check their alibis for her own peace of mind. She quickly received a message back confirming that all four families had been with her all evening. She also said she was looking forward to seeing Malice at the All Hallows' Haunt, wherever it ended up being held. This reminded Malice of the MacNe'erdoowells and Mordacious's less than gracious "congratulations" gift to Ma.

They left the four heads of the snubbed Topunder families on much better terms than when they'd found them. Malice promised that when (she hoped) they had cleared her parents of ghostnapping, she would speak to them about opening up the invitation to include all the Topunder families. And they in turn had offered to act as character witnesses for Ma and

Pa should the need arise, though Malice sincerely hoped it wouldn't.

"That's four suspects crossed off the list in one fell swoop," said Uncle Vex, liberally puffing perfume on to his hair with an atomizer bulb he kept in his jacket pocket. "So, all in all, definitely worth the headlock, though I fear I shall be haunted by the scent of Stinky's armpit for some time to come."

Malice wished she felt better about narrowing down her list of suspects. If she was honest with herself, she was worried that they would run out of suspects to pursue and her parents would be convicted for a crime they didn't commit.

22

NO WONKY WISHES FROM THE WITCHES

"I think we should visit the Shipton witches," said Malice as they walked along Shifty Row, munching on the cakes Seth had produced from his rucksack.

"Is that really necessary?" asked Uncle Vex.

Uncle Vex was, to put it bluntly, frightened of witches. He would tell you it wasn't fear he had; it was an allergy to witches – but everyone knew it wasn't true.

"They've always helped me before," Malice

reasoned. "And I just have this feeling in my gut that they can help us."

"Guts again!" sighed Uncle Vex.

"Well, we haven't had any news back about the MacNe'erdoowells yet, so we might as well keep gathering intel," Malice reasoned.

So far as anyone knew, the MacNe'erdoowells were still in Edinburgh and probably at that moment racing to prepare for the All Hallows' Haunt. Uncle Vex had put out some feelers with contacts he had in the north, and they were waiting for news.

"Are we going to the witches' shop?" asked Seth. "I've always wanted to see inside the Be-Careful-What-You-Wish-For Emporium."

"Yes," said Malice, "but don't get any ideas about buying a wish. They never turn out how you expect."

"How do you mean?"

Malice shifted her sister on to her other hip as they walked.

"Say you wished to be rich," Malice began. "Well, the word 'rich' has lots of definitions; it can mean lots of money, or a luxurious fabric or rich foods like oil and double cream … you might end up as a block of butter!"

"Oh, that would be very rich," Uncle Vex agreed. "Too much butter gives me heartburn."

"But as far as the witches are concerned," Malice continued, "they would have fulfilled your wish. Maybe you would wish to be the fastest runner in the world, and then you turn into a cheetah. It's still a wish fulfilled."

"I was going to wish to be taller," said Seth.

"No!" said Uncle Vex and Malice at the same time.

"I can't even imagine what that wish would look like – you'd probably turn into a giant," said Uncle Vex. "Your dads would have to build a house the size of Big Ben just to fit you in it. No, old chap, take the advice. No wonky wishes from the witches."

Seth puffed out a disappointed, "All right!"

It was almost four o'clock and fully dark by the time they had doubled back to the Haunting Quarter. Luckily, they had managed to catch a ghost-tram most of the way, which had delighted Antipathy-Rose but not so much the conductor when he realized she had eaten his bell.

The dark brought with it thoughts of Ma and Pa facing a night in the Underland prison – the first of many if they couldn't fathom who had framed them – and once again Malice's heart felt heavy. But as the warm lights of the Be-Careful-What-You-Wish-For Emporium came into view, Malice began to feel more hopeful.

As Malice reached for the door handle, Uncle Vex stepped forward.

"Let me take my little shark-toothed niece for a while," he said. And then, more quietly, to himself: "They're less likely to hex a man with a baby."

By contrast, Seth was hopping on the spot with
excitement to get in.

The Emporium was laid out in long thin aisles
with floor to ceiling shelves which held row upon row
of vials glooping dangerously with waiting wishes.
Each aisle offered a different wish theme and was
labelled accordingly: Revenge, Wealth, Vanity, Pox,
Painful Truths, Nightmares, Secrets. The genres and
their sub-genres seemed to go on endlessly. Some

of the vials sparkled, others glowed ominously and some pulsated with unnerving energy. The air was full of the whispers which emitted from the vials: soft cajoling voices making promises they wouldn't keep and tempting shoppers to part with their money for tainted wishes.

Seth was mesmerized. Literally. He wandered as though in a trance towards a shelf where a navy-blue vial called softly to him. He reached out his hand to touch the vial, whispering dreamily, "Yes, I can hear you. Of course I'd like to be your friend, that would be lovely…"

Malice grabbed his hand away just in time.

"Not so fast, wish-boy!" she said, shaking her friend by the shoulders.

Seth's eyes refocused and he shook his head.

"Woah, what just happened?" he asked.

"You were mesmerized," Malice replied.

"How embarrassing," said Seth.

"Don't worry about it." Malice gave her friend a quick hug. "This kind of magic is hard for Topsiders to resist."

She linked her arm through his and walked towards the counter. Uncle Vex followed behind, crouching low and hugging Antipathy-Rose to his chest. The witches were stirring a huge bubbling cauldron and they looked up, grinning, as Malice approached.

"There she be," said Pestilence.

"Just as told," added Blight.

"Curious and lion bold," finished Miasma.

"Hello," Malice greeted the witches. "You remember my friend, Seth?"

The witches narrowed their eyes and nodded.

"Ever thought about wrapping yourself in pastry?" Blight asked Seth.

"Erm…" Seth replied.

"Mmmm." Miasma nodded. "Maybe coating yourself in a rich mushroom duxelles."

"Seth Wellington, with a thick gravy," added Pestilence.

"Seth is not on the menu," said Malice, standing her tallest. "Don't make me tell Nana Rascally on you."

Nana Rascally was kind of a big deal in witchy circles. The witches looked peeved but pulled their eyes away from Seth.

"We were only joking," Blight addressed Seth. "It's just a little witch humour, that's all." She smiled wickedly at Seth and he stepped back out of grabbing reach, just in case.

"I've been wanting to talk with you," said Malice.

"We know," said Pestilence.

"That's why you're here!" added Blight.

"To speak to our collective ear," finished Miasma.

"What do you know about the mayor's ghostnap?" asked Malice.

"We knows she ain't napped no more."

"We knows it weren't to even no score."

"You need to find the reason at its core," said the witches in unison.

Malice thought for a moment.

"Are you saying that whoever framed my parents

didn't do it to get revenge?"

"Not revenge," Blight mused, "so much as clearing a path."

"To cause a distraction you first need a ruse," said Miasma.

"So many frenemies from which to choose," added Pestilence.

"A ghostnap's just right to deflect and confuse," finished Blight.

"So," Malice was thinking out loud, "the ghostnapping wasn't the point at all, and the ransom note was just a dead herring because someone wanted my parents out of the way?"

"She's quick as a whip and sharp as a tack!" quipped Pestilence.

"But what for?" Malice asked. "It seems unlikely that Ma and Pa would want to hamper any mischief that was going down – they'd more likely want to be a part of it!"

"Unless it was a mischief that the villains didn't want to share with your parents?" Seth suggested.

"Good old-fashioned greed!" called Uncle Vex from behind a stand of vials.

"What, like a treasure hoard?" Malice asked.

Seth shrugged.

"Maybe," he said. "It seems like as good a reason as revenge to frame someone."

"Yes, I suppose it is," Malice agreed. Then she turned her attention back to the witches and asked, "Is this about treasure?"

"That depends on your definition of treasure."

"Is gold your fancy or is power your pleasure?"

"One man's jackpot is another man's junk."

"Not all relics are found in a trunk."

While Malice was mulling this over, Seth jumped in.

"Do you actually know who did it?"

The witches baulked.

"Brave for a Topsider!"

"Candid, too."

"I wonder what he'd taste like in a stew?"

Malice placed herself in front of Seth.

"Ladies, please, it's very rude to threaten to eat customers."

"He hasn't bought anything!" challenged Blight. "So, he ain't no customer!"

"If I might draw your attention to the lanyard around the young man's neck," called Uncle Vex from behind a giant cardboard cut-out of the three shop witches. "You'll see he is under my protection."

The witches cackled derisively.

"Vendetta Grudge was right about him," said Pestilence.

"Yeah," cackled Blight. "All bubbles but no bottle!"

"Rude!" Uncle Vex called from his hiding place.

But Malice had homed in on something else.

"When did you see Vendetta Grudge?" she asked.

"Last night, down the King's Head pub," said Blight. "We had a meeting."

Malice's mind was suddenly whirring. Could the Grudges have something to do with this mess? Surely not, they were her parents' closest allies, after all. They'd stood up for them in court. Or at least, they'd tried to. Hadn't they? But all the same…

"Was your meeting just with Vendetta or was Animosity there too?" Malice asked.

"They was both there," said Pestilence. "Like a pair of grinning hyenas; charm so slick you could slip on it."

"What time was your meeting?"

"Six forty-five," said Miasma.

"And what time did the Grudges leave?" asked Seth from behind Malice's shoulder. He had picked up her chain of thought.

"A quarter past seven," said Pestilence. "I remember because that gave us fifteen minutes

to jump on our brooms and get back for the latest episode of Abdication Street on the wireless."

"And they never left your sight?" Malice asked. She knew she was clutching at bones, but she had to ask.

"Not once."

"Nor twice," added Miasma.

"Or even thrice," finished Pestilence.

"Well, that seems to settle it," said Uncle Vex, who had taken cover behind an obsidian statue of Hecate. "Mayor Dawdle heard her clock chime 7 p.m. just before she was ghostnapped. That rules out the Grudges as suspects."

"I suppose I'm relieved," said Malice thoughtfully. "I don't much like any of the Grudges, but my parents do, in their own way, and it would be a horrible betrayal if it had been them."

Seth popped his head around Malice's shoulder again.

"Would it be rude to ask what your meeting was

about?" he asked. "I'm just curious."

"I like his audacity," said Blight. "He knows curiosity ate the cat, but he keeps poking the beast just the same."

"We like a tenacious Topsider," agreed Pestilence, "and not just with chips!"

"Because we admire your gutsy nature, we'll answer your question," added Miasma. "The Grudges want to buy the emporium. Apparently, they want to go into retail."

"Really?" Malice exclaimed. "I didn't know you were selling."

"We're not! And, in no uncertain terms, we told the blighters so."

"This is more than just a business. It's a calling, don't you know?"

"What seems rotten on the surface hides a danger way beneath."

"Sometimes it takes a witch's guile to protect

against a thief."

Malice let the words run around in her head and settle into an order.

"You don't want the emporium to fall into the wrong hands," Malice clarified.

"Precisely!" agreed Miasma. "And the Grudges' hands are definitely wrong'uns!"

This made sense. The Grudges were unscrupulous at best. Malice doubted they could be trusted with an emporium full of wayward wishes – who knew what trouble they could create!

CATCH THAT BABY!

"Would you like to hear a riddle?" asked Pestilence.

"As if we haven't heard enough!" whispered Uncle Vex loudly from behind a cabinet displaying shrunken heads.

Malice ignored him.

"I would love to," said Malice. She pulled out her notebook and waited, pen poised.

The witches began in unison.

"When time is never on your side
    it's hard to spot the trick.
On its face, time ticks for Tardy,
    or does it go tock-tick?
Forwards, backwards, what a blunder,
    the hands of time are forced.
Reluctant rogue, poor shy Topunder,
    a quest to be endorsed.
A consultation taken with a side
    order of ruse,
Hides a wrong pinned on to rivals
    with indubitable clues.
It takes a cunning plan to be in
    two places at a time,
With witnesses to prove that you
    were nowhere near the crime.
A lie is made more sturdy when
    it's camouflaged in fact,
Dispute each truth, unpick the
    proof, leave no alibi intact."

The witches looked very pleased with themselves. Malice knew better than to try and fathom their riddles straight off; she often needed time to ruminate on them before their meaning fell into focus. The final few lines, though, gave Malice pause for thought: *A lie is made more sturdy when it's camouflaged in fact. Dispute each truth, unpick the proof, leave no alibi intact.* Perhaps all the cast-iron alibis they had met with were *not* so watertight – all they had to do was find the crack.

"Thank you," said Malice. "That was very riddly."

The witches grinned, showing cracked, blackened teeth.

A shrill voice rang out through the emporium, *BITE, BITE, BITE, BITE!*

"I can't hold her any longer!" called Uncle Vex. "She's eaten my favourite handkerchief and bitten through both my sock suspenders!"

Grinning with mischief, Antipathy-Rose toddled

out from behind the statue of Hecate and with surprising speed began to weave in and out of the aisles.

"Putrid Pumpkins!" shouted Malice. "If she bites through a wish vial, we're *all* in trouble!"

"Catch that baby!" called Uncle Vex, his fear of witches vanishing as the greater threat of a toddler in a wish store dawned.

"She's too quick!" called Seth from the Revenge aisle. "It's like she's on roller skates!"

"She's climbing over the Vanity aisle!" called Malice. "Try and catch her in the Hex aisle!"

Remarkably, Antipathy-Rose hadn't managed to smash a single vial, even now as she ran along the

top of the Life & Death aisle, her little shoes clomping. The vials wobbled dangerously but didn't fall.

"She's crawling underneath Curses! I can't reach her!" cried Uncle Vex.

"Why don't the witches help us?" shouted Seth frustratedly. "Cast a spell or something, it's *their* shop!"

"We're enjoying the show!" shouted Blight.

"Just look at her go!" cackled Pestilence.

"It could all end in woe!" squawked Miasma delightedly.

Malice dashed along the aisles, desperately trying to second-guess where her sister would toddle next. It was like playing whack-a-mole – she kept disappearing and then popping up again where you'd least expect her.

Out of the corner of her eye, Malice caught a flash of Antipathy-Rose's pink hair ribbon. She stopped and listened, blocking out the whispers of the vials and the shouts of Seth and Uncle Vex. And then she heard it, little clippy-cloppy shoes and a sad voice calling, "Ma, Pa, Ma, Pa," over and over again. Malice

followed the sound up and down the aisles until she came to a sign which read: Deadly Secrets.

High above her, Malice's baby sister teetered on the top of the Deadly Secrets aisle. Her cheeks were crimson and tear-stained, and Malice's heart broke to see Antipathy-Rose so sad, until she saw the dark green bubbling vial in her hand, and Malice's sadness turned to terror.

"Anti, come down from there, there's my mangy maggot," Malice cajoled.

Antipathy-Rose looked down at her. Her expression morphing between sad, angry and frightened. Malice couldn't blame her. No wonder she felt those things – she was so little, and when you're small and confused it's hard to know which feeling to feel first. Malice smiled kindly at her sister.

"Come on down for a cuddle and a rock cake," she said.

Antipathy-Rose looked from Malice to the vial

and back again, and then she speared the cork with her teeth and pulled out the stopper, spitting it down on to the floor below. She shouted, "MA, PA!" at the top of her voice and hurled the vial against the statue of Hecate. The vial splintered and the liquid inside exploded in red, green and black smoke.

The whole emporium shuddered; the vials clinked like the sound of a thousand chandeliers in an earthquake. Malice looked up through the smoke and saw Antipathy-Rose lose her balance and fall.

"No!" screamed Malice, just as Uncle Vex skidded across the floor with his arms outstretched and caught the toddler before she hit the ground. Antipathy-Rose giggled and kissed his nose. Malice swooped over and picked her sister up, hugging her so tightly and kissing her hot cheeks so many times that Antipathy-Rose laughed and squirmed in her arms.

"Is everyone OK?" Seth appeared out of the smoke, coughing but unharmed.

A crackling noise like frying bacon sounded above their heads and they all looked up at the statue of Hecate. Where the liquid had splattered against her obsidian chest, something new was appearing, knitting together, thin at first, almost transparent like gauze, but growing more robust as more layers knitted together. It grew until none of the liquid from the vial remained, but in its place was a tattered square of papyrus, which unstuck itself from Hecate's chest and floated down through the smoky air. Seth reached out and gently caught it, holding it out for all of them to see.

"It's a map," said Malice.

"A map of Underland," Uncle Vex confirmed.

Malice turned to the witches, who were just becoming visible again through the smoke.

"Did my sister make a wish?" she asked them.

"In her own way," said Miasma.

Malice bit her lip.

"Will it, you know, go wonky, like all the other

wishes?" she asked, worrying what the implications for her sister would be.

Blight smiled a smile which reminded Malice of Nana Rascally.

"Worry ye not, child," she soothed. "A wish from a guileless heart will never be harmful. Though it may hold a truth well disguised."

"But that's where you come in," said Pestilence. "You are a truth-seeker, Malice Morbid."

"And in finding the truth you will get the wish which both your hearts desire," added Miasma.

"Ma and Pa," said Malice, but the witches only shrugged and stirred their cauldron.

"And now we request that you bid us farewell."

"Vamoose! See ya later, no longer to dwell."

"The witching hour comes, and we plan to raise hell!"

The three witches raised their hands to their lips and blew kisses at Uncle Vex, Seth, Malice and

Antipathy-Rose. The kisses landed like a shove from
a silverback gorilla and pushed them all the way out
of the emporium, their shoes and boots squeaking on

the tiles as they skidded. The door opened with a ting-a-ling, and they were deposited in a heap outside the shop. The door locked itself behind them, the shutters clamped down at the windows with a clatter and the "open" sign flipped itself to "closed" with a rather rude raspberry sound.

"Phew!" Seth exclaimed as they dusted themselves down. "I think we got off lightly there. I thought they were going to turn us into frogs for making a mess in their shop!"

"That's such a misconception," Malice chided him, smiling.

"What? Are you saying witches don't turn people into frogs?"

"Hardly ever!" said Malice. "They're far more likely to turn you into something useful like a chicken or a Hoover. Witches are very practical women!"

"Practical, yes. Gentle at giving one the old heave-ho, not so much," grumbled Uncle Vex, looking at the

scuffs on the backs of his shoes with a sorrowful face. "These are Italian – ghost-made," he muttered. "One of a kind. My shoemaker will be so disappointed."

FOXES HAVE VERY LITTLE USE FOR MONEY

They made their way hastily out of the Haunting Quarter and on to the safer streets of the Shadow District. The Haunting Quarter was the kind of place you kept your wits about you during the day and kept well away from at night.

Antipathy-Rose needed her dinner, and they were all pretty hungry, so they dropped into Lethal Legumes, the vegan café owned by Vlad and Lilith the vegan vampires. Malice pulled a pair of sunglasses out

of her pinafore pocket and handed them to Seth. The last time he had seen Lilith he had been accidentally glamoured by her, and Belladonna had needed to fix him an anti-glamour potion. It wasn't Lilith's fault; Topsiders have no immunity to vampire glamours.

"How lovely to see you!" Lilith fussed around them all, getting them settled at a table. "It's been too long. You mustn't leave it such an age next time!"

"What can I get you today, my fine friends?" asked Vlad. "Our specials are the dandelion ravioli and it's two for one on spinach lattes."

They gave their orders and Vlad went off to prepare them. Lilith sat down at their table, bouncing Antipathy-Rose on her knee and cooing over her.

"Look at her teeth! Vlad, have you seen the baby's teeth? Oh my, they are gloriously sharp. Can they cut through tin?" she asked Malice.

"Oh, yes," said Malice proudly. "She's been opening food cans since she was tiny. Pa's just started her on

scaffolding poles and she's doing really well; she'll be on steel girders in no time!"

"We have a children's play cage at the back of the shop. It's got a cannonball pit and chain-mail climbing wall, and we've just installed a knife-throwing range. Do you think your sister would like it?"

"She'd love it!" said Malice. "She could do with a bit of play time – she's been dragged round Underland with us all day."

"I heard about your parents," said Vlad solemnly, as he placed their food down on the table. "I've known your Pa for many years; he is bad but not to the bone. I hope you find who did this to them."

"Thank you, Vlad," said Malice.

Lilith took Antipathy-Rose off to the play cage and the others discussed the case as they ate.

"I don't think we should be disheartened," said Uncle Vex. "We've managed to cross several Topunders off our suspect list."

"And a couple that weren't even *on* the suspect list," Seth added.

"You mean the Grudges," said Malice, and Seth nodded.

"And there's that note you found with the invisible ink," added Seth.

"Well, it might not be connected to the case," said Malice.

"Oh, I think it fits in there somewhere. Plus, we've gathered hair and paint samples from the crime scene," put in Uncle Vex.

"*One* of the crime scenes," said Malice. "I'd really like to take a look in Mayor Dawdle's study. I doubt

Chief Braggart has bothered looking for evidence since he thinks he's got this case in the bag."

"Mmmmm," Uncle Vex pondered. "You're right about that. Maybe you should send a moth-mail and see if it's convenient for us to pay her a visit after we've eaten."

Malice nodded and began to whisper a moth-calling spell. After a few seconds, a flutter of skeletal winged moths flittered into the café like a cloud of elderflower blossom and encircled Malice's head. She smiled as their delicate wings tickled her nose and brushed her cheeks. When she had given her message, the moths rose as one, like confetti on a breeze, and fluttered out.

"Now," said Uncle Vex, spreading the old map out on the table, "we need to decipher what this map means."

"What makes you think it means anything?" asked Seth.

"Because, old bean, when young Anti-R made

237

her rudimentary wish, she called out for her parents. We can presume from that that she misses them and wished to have them back. The wish therefore would be bound to provide a way for that to happen. In this instance, I think it's fair to say that this is a clue to prove their innocence. If only we can work out how."

The map was brown with age and had been torn and fixed more than once. The creases in the papyrus were deep, like very old skin, and some of the ink had blurred. Now that they could see it more closely, they saw that it didn't chart the whole of Underland, just the parts under London – the parts Malice knew best. She looked at the map from every which way, but it was just an old map. No X marks the spot, no arrows, nothing that looked like any kind of clue.

Malice was saved from feeling too disheartened by the return of her moth-mail and a message from the mayor inviting them round at their earliest convenience.

"Seth, old boy, do you think you ought to send a moth-mail to your dads telling them you'll be staying for a sleepover tonight? I don't want them to worry," said Uncle Vex.

"I think they'll worry more if a cloud of moths starts fluttering around their heads," Seth replied.  "They're pretty open-minded but they have their limits. And anyway, they don't speak Moth."

Uncle Vex tutted.

"You're quite right, of course. You're so much a part of the family, I forget sometimes that you're not actually a Topunder."

Seth smiled so broadly at this that Malice worried his mouth would swallow his head. His cheeks beamed red with pride.

"I'll see if old Vlad's got a computer I can send a ghoulagram on to keep your dads in the loop," said Uncle Vex. "Oh, and Malice, I'm expecting a message back from my contacts about the MacNe'erdoowells' movements. I wasn't sure where we'd be, so I asked them to send it via night creature, it's easier that way. You don't mind translating, do you?"

"Not at all," answered Malice.

Uncle Vex left the table in search of Vlad, and Antipathy-Rose could be heard squealing with delight in the cannonball pit. It was the first time Seth and Malice had been on their own since that morning.

"How are you holding up, bestie?" Seth asked, pushing his sunglasses back up his nose.

"OK," said Malice. "There are just so many loose ends at the moment – we've got riddles and clues and evidence but none of it seems to tie together in any way."

"You know how these things go; it only takes one clue to suddenly link all the others together. We just haven't found it yet."

"But will we find it in time, Seth? I'm starting to wonder."

"Of course we will. It's like doing a jigsaw – you can't make a whole picture until you've got all the pieces. We haven't finished gathering yet – we've still got the MacNe'erdoowells and the mayor to visit."

"You sound like Grandad," Malice laughed.

"I might have stolen the jigsaw line from him." Seth grinned sheepishly.

The bell above the café door chimed and a fox slinked in and parked itself next to Malice.

"Hello," said Malice. "Are you here for me?"

The fox nodded.

"Is it Uncle Vex's information?"

The fox nodded again.

Malice took out her notebook and pencil.

"You don't mind if I write it down, do you?"

She couldn't be sure, but she thought the fox shrugged its shoulders in a

"Whatever" kind of way.

Malice leaned down with her ear to the fox's mouth and the fox began to relay the message. Foxes' voices are low and husky but at the same time smooth, like the sound of a broom swishing fallen leaves or a wave receding from a pebbly shore. This fox was called Agog. He happened to be the cousin of a fox Malice was friendly with in the grounds of Malignant House, called Avid. Agog was not quite so friendly as Avid, but he delivered his message quickly and efficiently and Malice gave him her leftover ravioli as a tip; foxes have very little use for money.

Uncle Vex came back and threw himself down in the chair.

"All done, old boy. Your dads are happy for you to have a sleepover and they've invited me over for dinner next week. Bill's got a new invention he wants me to look over."

Seth rolled his eyes.

Malice felt pleased. Since her uncle and Bill had met again after so many years, they had rekindled their old friendship. Uncle Vex went over for dinner every couple of weeks and the thought of it made Malice happy. It was good for him; he needed a distraction, or he'd work all day and all night, and she knew he felt lonely sometimes down in Underland. Not that he didn't have lots of the undead as friends, but sometimes you just need to converse with another human. And, of course, relations had thawed significantly with Ma and Pa too, and she knew that meant a great deal to both Pa and Uncle Vex.

"Did I just see a ravioli munching fox leaving the building?" Uncle Vex asked.

"Yes. He was the messenger," Malice began. "He said the MacNe'erdoowells travelled down from Edinburgh last week and have been staying at the Burke and Hare B&B."

"Hmmm," Uncle Vex mused, twirling his quiff.

"Did they just fancy a holiday ahead of the All Hallows' Haunt or were they masterminding a plot to frame your parents for the mayor's ghostnapping?"

"That remains to be seen," said Malice. "The manager of the B&B told your informant that the MacNe'erdoowells plan to leave tonight to go back to Edinburgh, since they've been tasked with hosting the All Hallows' Haunt in place of my parents. We need to speak with them before they leave," said Malice, with sudden urgency. She was feeling very much that time was slipping through their fingers.

"Calm yourself, old girl. I'll send a ghoulagram now and arrange a meeting with them for 7 p.m. That will give us plenty of time to pay our visit to Mayor Dawdle and catch the MacNe'erdoowells before they leave town."

And off he dashed to use Vlad's computer again.

They settled their bill and, with some difficulty, extracted Antipathy-Rose from the cannonball

pit, where many of the balls were now the size of ball-bearings.

"Sorry about that," said Malice meekly. "She likes to whittle things."

Vlad waved a dismissive hand and smiled, his fangs glinting in the candlelight.

"We've all been there!" he said knowingly.

PUSTULE GREEN
NUMBER FIVE

Mayor Dawdle lived in a flat overlooking the garden
of the Burke and Hare B&B, a coincidence which
was not lost on Malice. The mayor managed to look
harassed and windswept as she led them up to her flat.

"It's grisly to see you again," she puffed, as though
she had just been running. Even as she made them
cups of tea, she whirled about the kitchen at top
speed, opening and closing cupboards with such
rapidity that Malice's hair was blown about by the

breeze. Malice felt tired just watching her.

They took tea in Tardy's study, the scene of the crime.

"Was anything taken when you were ghostnapped?" asked Uncle Vex, carefully making his way around the chaotic office with his magnifying glass.

"Nothing," Tardy replied.

"And you didn't notice anything unusual in the lead up to it?" Malice asked.

"No one lurking about?" added Seth.

"No," said Tardy, taking a sip of her tea.

"Nothing at all out of the ordinary?" Malice pressed.

The mayor sucked in her cheeks as though she was mulling something over, wondering whether or not to bring it up.

"Anything at all," Malice encouraged. "Sometimes the smallest detail can be the thing that cracks the case."

"It's such a little thing," the mayor began.

Malice felt a flicker of hope in her chest.

"It hardly seems worth mentioning. And yet, at the same time, I simply don't have an explanation for it. You'll think I'm silly."

"I promise we won't," said Malice. "Whatever it is, if it's playing on your mind then it's important."

The mayor smiled gratefully.

"It's my grandfather clock," she began. "Or rather, the key to my grandfather clock. You see, I have a tendency to be a little absent-minded. With that in mind, I have certain things that I keep to a strict routine. It helps, you see, if you're scatterbrained like me, to repeat

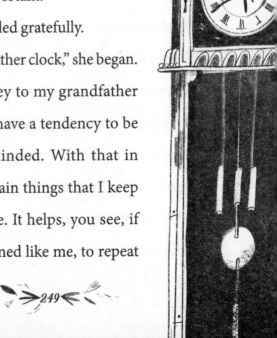

the same processes over and over. That grandfather clock was passed down to me by my father and it's my most prized possession. I have been winding it since I was a girl. I keep the key to the clockface in the glass dish on the console table in the hall. Once a week, on a Thursday at 6 p.m. without fail, I use the key to open the clock face and wind it; it's the only thing I'm never late for. But last night the key wasn't in the glass dish."

"Where was it?" asked Malice.

Uncle Vex and Seth had stopped their clue searches to listen.

"It was in the lock. But you see, I wouldn't have left it there. I never do. I never have. Someone had put the key in the lock, and it wasn't me."

"And you're sure that nothing else at all was moved or stolen?" asked Uncle Vex, though Malice wondered, in all that clutter, how the mayor would be able to tell.

"I am sure," she said. "It may look like chaos, but I can assure you, it is organized chaos."

Malice noted the moved key down in her notebook. Seth went back to helping Uncle Vex look for clues, holding open small brown envelopes for any potential evidence.

"This mud?" Uncle Vex said, pointing to a clod of dried earth on the carpet. "Do you know where it came from?"

"Oh, that'll be from my trainers. I like an early morning run before my breakfast meetings."

Uncle Vex nodded.

"Do you run every morning?" Malice asked.

"Yes, regular as clockwork."

"What's this?" Seth asked.

They all four bent to inspect a thumbnail sized fleck of something on the carpet by the mayor's chair.

"Looks like paint," said Uncle Vex, plucking it up with his tweezers and dropping it into the

waiting envelope. "Pustule Green Number Five of the Underland Colour Chart if I'm not mistaken. Interesting, especially since that colour was discontinued in 1880."

"I found paint flecks in Ma's office too," said Malice. The cogs of her mind were beginning to turn at last and Malice was greatly relieved. She had been wondering if she'd lost her mystery-solving-mojo.

"Do you have a cat?" asked Seth.

"No, I'm allergic," said the mayor.

Malice crossed to where Seth was scooping short stubby gingery hairs off a cushion and into an evidence envelope.

"Maybe the ghostnapper brought this in on their clothes?" she suggested. "It's almost the same colour as the hairs I found back at home."

"Very possibly," Uncle Vex agreed.

They spent some time working their way around the flat, looking for clues which might have been

dropped by the ghostnappers as they manhandled poor Tardy through her home. Antipathy-Rose crawled along beside them, biting chunks out of skirting boards and door frames as she went. They found several more paint flecks and some more short hairs which had got caught in the "Not Welcome" mat. The mayor had just offered more tea when the grandfather clock began to chime.

"Great Golems!" Uncle Vex exclaimed. "Seven o'clock already!"

"We're late!" Malice cried in alarm. She really didn't want to miss her chance to interview the MacNe'erdoowells before they left for Edinburgh.

"Never fear, young apprentice, we are but moments from the Burke and Hare, we'll be no more than five minutes late, and that's a promise!"

They left Mayor Tardy Dawdle in the kind of whirling fluster that she would have been proud of. Malice wondered fleetingly if being late was catching. Out of the corner of her eye, Malice caught sight of someone ducking down behind a hedge. It was only a brief glance, but Malice could have sworn it was Maudlin Grudge. However, when they reached the hedge there was no one there. She chided herself. It was just her eyes playing tricks on her in the dark.

DID WE FALL INTO A
TIME WORMHOLE?

They found the MacNe'erdoowells fuming outside
the B&B surrounded by a pile of travelling trunks.
A horse and carriage stood on the cobbled road. The
horse brayed impatiently, white steam pluming out
from its nostrils and up into the cold night.

"Greetings and salutations!" said Uncle Vex.

"Are you pulling our chain?" snarled Truculent
MacNe'erdoowell, rolling his wheelchair backwards
and forwards in agitation.

"Excuse me?" Uncle Vex looked confused.

"Do you think our time is not precious?" snapped Mordacious.

"We won't be kept hanging around by the likes of you!" added Truculent.

Malice guessed that, unlike Mayor Dawdle, the MacNe'erdoowells must be sticklers for time.

"My dear people, I apologize sincerely for keeping you waiting. We did, admittedly, lose track of time,

but we left at the strike of seven and ran all the way, so we are only three minutes late, four at the most."

"We are sorry," said Malice.

"Very sorry," added Seth.

"Bite!" said Antipathy-Rose.

"Three minutes?" screeched Mordacious.

"Try thirty!" added Truculent.

Uncle Vex chuckled amiably and pulled out his pocket watch.

"I beg to differ," he said, as he flipped open the case. "The time is… Oh!"

"What is it?" asked Malice.

"According to my watch, it's thirty-six minutes past seven."

"That can't be right," said Malice. "Mayor Dawdle's grandfather clock just struck seven!"

"Clearly not!" said Truculent, thrumming his fingers on the arm of his chair.

"Did we fall into a time wormhole?" asked Seth.

"I've read about those. And nothing would surprise me down here."

"Are you deliberately holding us up so that we can't organize the All Hallows' Haunt? Is that what this is?" asked Mordacious.

"Jealousy, plain and simple," added Truculent. "Typical Maligns."

Malice stepped forward and held her hands out placatingly.

"We honestly are not trying to hold you up. I'm really sorry that we're late. I can't explain what's happened. Yet," she added, because a bud of an idea was beginning to unfurl inside her mind. "All we wanted to do was to rule you out of our list of suspects."

"Suspects?" asked Truculent.

"I don't believe that my parents ghostnapped the mayor or had any intention of robbing the Underland Bank."

"We think they were framed," Seth chimed in.

Truculent looked up at Mordacious.

"You were right," he said to her.

Mordacious sighed. "Told you!" And then, turning to the three investigators, she said, "I agree with you."

Malice, Seth and Uncle Vex's mouths all dropped open at the same time.

"You do?" asked Uncle Vex.

"It's just not their style," Mordacious said, shrugging.

"We enjoy, what you might call, a healthy mistrust and pleasant loathing with Pugnacious and Tetchy-Sue," Truculent explained. "We've been frenemies for years."

"We know all their sneaky mischief moves," agreed Mordacious. "They are low-down louses but they're no ghostnappers. If they were going to rob a bank they'd do it quietly, strictly under the radar, none of this singing and dancing ransom nonsense."

"But if you knew they didn't do it, you could have come forward as character witnesses," said Malice.

"With what evidence?" asked Truculent. "Whoever's set them up has set them up good."

"And if we went in there shouting their innocence, we'd be directing attention to ourselves," Mordacious added. "We're hardly going to drop ourselves in the soup, are we? Our being here is suspicious enough as it is."

"That reminds me," said Uncle Vex. "Why *are* you here?"

Mordacious looked at the ground.

"You might as well tell them," said Truculent in a resigned voice.

"It was meant to be a surprise." Mordacious couldn't look them in the eye. "I was jealous when your parents were awarded the All Hallows' Haunt. We've had a lovely time lording it over them for the last few years and it didn't feel good that they suddenly had the upper hand."

Mordacious stopped, seeming reluctant to go on.

"So, that's why you sent Ma a bouquet of flowers with the heads on," Malice prompted.

Mordacious nodded. "I realized I'd overstepped the mark of common indecency as soon as I'd sent them. But it was too late."

"Flowers with their heads on," Truculent muttered under his breath. "Sometimes you go too far, my petty-poophead."

"I know," said Mordacious, taking Truculent's hand. "I wanted to make it up to her. So, we came down early, ahead of the ball, to book the Festering Zombie Dance Troupe. They were going to turn up as a surprise at the All Hallows' Haunt and do an impromptu routine."

"Ma would've loved that," Malice said. She had a lump in her throat and had to swallow it hard to keep from crying.

"She would," agreed Uncle Vex. "There's never

been a more stinky act."

"The way their rotting limbs fly off into the crowd during the can-can," said Truculent, smiling. "There's nothing else like it. It's Art, plain and simple."

"So, now you know," said Mordacious, her cheeks burning with shame. "I'm nothing but a filthy sentimentalist."

"We were trying to keep a low profile. Obviously kind deeds are not the sort of thing we want to get a reputation for. Though, to be honest, we wondered if the jig was up when the Grudge boy caught us doing Spook-Chi in the garden," said Truculent, shaking his head. "The Grudges are worse gossips than the ghosts."

Suddenly Malice was alert.

"The Grudge boy?" she asked. "Do you mean Maudlin Grudge?"

"Yeah, that's him."

So maybe it was him she'd just seen behind the

hedge. But what was he doing in Underland, alone in the dark?

"You saw him here, in Underland?" Malice asked urgently.

"Yes."

"When?"

"Every bloomin' morning!" said Truculent.

"We like to do early morning Spook-Chi – it's ever so good, a zen workout for mind and body!" Mordacious began. "Anyway, we didn't want to break our routine, so we did it in Burke and Hare's garden while we were here. Well, that Maudlin was like clockwork. We'd start our routine, wave at the mayor over the hedge when she went off for her morning run and then, ten minutes later, the Grudge boy would run past in the other direction. Not a chatty child but there's nothing wrong with that."

"Could you see where he was coming from?" asked Seth.

"Or where he was going to?" asked Uncle Vex.

Mordacious and Truculent shrugged.

"How long have you been staying here?" Malice queried.

"Eight days," said Truculent. "It took us a bit of time to organize things with the zombies – they're pretty booked up."

"And you saw Maudlin every day?"

Mordacious thought for a moment.

"Not quite," she replied. "We didn't seem him on the first morning, and he definitely wasn't there today."

"So, you saw him run past the hedge six days in a row?" Malice confirmed.

Truculent and Mordacious nodded.

"I think I know how it was done!" said Malice. "Although proving it won't be easy," she muttered to herself. "And I still don't know why. Thank you! Thank you both so much!" she gushed, shaking first

Truculent and then Mordacious by the hand.

The MacNe'erdoowells looked uneasy.

"Keep it down, will you," Truculent hissed. "I don't want the Underlanders thinking we're do-gooders!"

"Yes, of course, sorry," said Malice, taking a step back and shouting, "Thanks for nothing, you down and dirty delinquents!"

Mordacious smiled. "Thanks, Malice," she whispered, and Truculent gave her a conspiratorial wink.

IN SPITE OF HERSELF,
SHE WAS HAVING FUN

With the MacNe'erdoowells on their way back to
Edinburgh. Malice, Antipathy-Rose, Seth and Uncle
Vex headed to the Investigations office so that Malice
could explain her theory. But as they rounded a
corner, Malice got a whiff of something familiar.

"Can you smell that?" she asked.

The others sniffed the air.

"Nope," said Seth. "Nothing other than the usual
Underland stinks."

"Me neither," added Uncle Vex.

Malice looked at her little sister, whose eyes had suddenly filled with tears.

"You can smell it, can't you, Anti," Malice said kindly, nuzzling her sister and holding her close.

"Ma!" wailed Antipathy-Rose.

"She's right," said Malice. "It's the smell of Ma's new stink-bomb juice."

"Why would it be down here?" asked Uncle Vex.

Malice concentrated hard, casting her mind back through the day's events, sifting through them to when she had last smelled that smell. And then it came to her, a vision of Animosity Grudge rubbing Ma's new stink-bomb juice into his beard and hair.

"The Grudges are nearby," she whispered. Adding, "Shhhhh!" and beckoning them to follow her.

"It doesn't matter where the Grudges are," Uncle Vex reasoned in a hissy whisper. "They still have a cast-iron alibi. They were with the Shipton witches when

the mayor was ghostnapped."

"But don't you think it's weird that they're down here sneaking around?" Malice challenged.

"To be fair, we're the ones who are sneaking around. The Grudges might just be out for a meal with friends," said Seth.

Malice knew the sense of what they were saying, but she also knew what her gut was saying, and it was telling her something was off.

They tiptoed along the quiet street, following the noses of Malice and Antipathy-Rose; the only sound was that of sniffing and the creak of Uncle Vex's very shiny shoes.

They were in a narrow side street, one of the many claustrophobic tributaries which weaved through the area. Malice looked around her, squinting into darkened doorways and peering through grimy windows. Ghosts glowered at the three investigators from beneath hooded cloaks and hurried on their way.

Malice let her nose guide her and followed the pong down another dismal alleyway. The pungent scent became stronger with every step until they found themselves standing in front of a decrepit tavern. The eerie glow from the dirty windows illuminated the alley in an ochre haze. The sign above them squeaked as it swung in an invisible breeze, the name read *The Poison Chalice*.

"Are you absolutely sure this is where your nose is leading you?" asked Uncle Vex, looking nervous. "Are you sure you aren't wishful sniffing?"

"Nope. This is where they are. I'm sure of it," said Malice.

"Is this one of those places Edna Cut-Throat said I might get eaten alive?" asked Seth.

Malice looked at her friend and bit her lip. She wanted to clear her parents' names but not at the cost of having her best friend devoured by Haunting Quarter ghouls.

"We need to stink you up a bit more – the more disgusting you smell, the better you'll fit in."

"This is the best day ever!" said Seth. And he wasn't even joking.

They looked about them. Something ominous was dribbling out of a downpipe on the wall.

"What about that?" Seth asked, excited.

Uncle Vex caught some of the sludge on his finger and inhaled. He gagged and wiped it on Seth's jacket.

"That ought to do it," he said, dabbing at his eyes with his handkerchief.

Seth stood under the downpipe and let the noxious goop dribble on to his head, giggling as it trickled down his neck. Malice rubbed it into his hair and styled it into a quiff not unlike Uncle Vex's. Uncle Vex

produced a pocket mirror from his pocket.

"Awesome!" said Seth. "How do I smell?"

"Nauseating!" said Uncle Vex. "You'll fit right in."

The tavern was low lit, and the clientele so absorbed in their own nefarious dealings they didn't notice as three private investigators and a toddler walked quietly through the bar. Malice smelled the Grudges before she saw them: the unmistakeable scent of stink bomb and yeti fur.

They were sitting at a table in a booth, separated by a wooden screen with stained-glass panels, heads pressed together in quiet conversation. Maudlin

sat opposite them looking glum. Malice and the others slipped into the booth next door and pressed as closely into the separating panel as they dared.

"You couldn't even get that right!" hissed Animosity. "What a

thing to forget!"

Maudlin sighed.

"I tried to fix it, but she had visitors," he replied.

"You'll just have to go back tomorrow morning, won't you?" sneered Vendetta. "We can't risk anyone finding out."

In Malice's head, the pieces of this puzzle were clicking into place. She was just a few shapes shy of a completed jigsaw.

"And you're no better!" Vendetta turned on her husband. "You should have burned the note as soon as you'd memorized it."

"Relax!" soothed Animosity. "Even if someone finds it, it won't mean anything to them. And without the blueprints it's worthless anyway."

BINGO!!! The last pieces of the puzzle slid into place inside her head and Malice had to cover her mouth to stop herself shouting "EUREKA!" in the middle of the Poison Chalice tavern. Instead, she

motioned with her head that they needed to get outside immediately.

They left as inconspicuously as they had arrived, weaving their way back through alleyways and backstreets until they came to a park. Malice hadn't dared to speak until they were away from prying eyes and straining ears. Uncle Vex and Seth were practically bursting at the seams with curiosity by the time they settled on a bench beneath a street lamp.

"Well?" demanded Uncle Vex. "I'm sure I don't know what it is that's got you so excited. It didn't sound like anything but their normal dodgy dealings to me!"

"Seth, could you get the map out, please?" Malice asked.

Seth pulled the map out of his rucksack and Malice opened her notebook and took out the piece of paper with the invisible ink.

"Uncle, is there any way we can heat this up so that

the writing shows through? I think the letters and numbers are coordinates."

Seth let out a whistle, which Antipathy-Rose tried to copy but ended up being a rather wet raspberry. Uncle Vex rooted around in his jacket and pulled out a pocket warmer.

"You really are a most remarkable Malign," exclaimed Uncle Vex, clicking the disc inside the handwarmer to activate the heat.

"What do you think it is?" asked Seth. "Treasure?"

"I would add a note of caution. This would appear to be a case quite separate to that of your parents," said Uncle Vex. "We are going off on a tangent. It's an interesting tangent, but a tangent none the less, and one we don't have the time for"

"But it could be the tangent that answers questions that could help my parents," said Malice. "Oh, I don't know. I just have this feeling that it's all connected. Like this is the final piece."

"Just because the Grudges are greedy, doesn't mean they are ghostnappers or people-framers," said Uncle Vex gently.

"I know," said Malice. "But I am going to prove to you that they are."

The handwarmer was toasty warm and Malice wrapped the note around it. It only took a few seconds for the writing to bloom across the page.

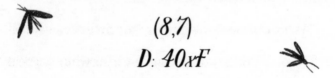

$$(8,7)$$
$$D: 40xF$$

Malice smoothed the map out and ran her finger across a line of numbers running along the bottom to the number eight. Another line of numbers ran vertically up the left-hand side. Seth moved his finger up to the number seven. And then they each ran their finger along their own line until their fingers met at the same point. Uncle Vex leaned in closer and let

out a small gasp.

"It's the building where your parents have their Haunting Agency office," he breathed.

"Which is the floor above the Be-Careful-What-What-You-Wish-For Emporium," added Malice.

"Didn't the witches say their meeting with the Grudges was about the Grudges wanting to buy their business?" asked Seth.

"Yes," agreed Malice. "They did."

"And didn't Belladonna say the Grudges were at the council breakfast meeting because they wanted planning or demolition permission, but she couldn't remember which?" piped up Uncle Vex, who rarely forgot anything Belladonna said to him.

"Yes," Malice agreed again. "But if they wanted to demolish the building, they'd have to buy my parents out too."

"So then, let us assume that demolition was not their goal," said Uncle Vex.

"If there's treasure under the emporium they don't need to tear the building down, they can just dig up the floor," agreed Malice.

"So, would the D stand for the depth they need to dig?" asked Seth.

"I would say so," Uncle Vex mused.

"But what's the F for?" asked Malice. "40Fs?"

Uncle Vex smoothed his hand over his panama hat.

"I would hazard a guess at *furlongs,*" he said. "It's an old Topunder measurement for distance."

"Is forty furlongs quite deep?" asked Seth.

"It's about five miles," said Uncle Vex.

"Quite deep then." Seth nodded.

"Who on earth, or in Underland, would bury treasure five miles down?" asked Malice. "It seems a bit excessive. Unless it was to ensure it would *never* be found."

"I'm just going to say that anything you want *never* to be found, probably isn't a good thing," said Seth.

"My sentiments exactly," said Uncle Vex, loosening his collar.

"Do you remember what the witches said when they told us about the Grudges wanting to buy the shop?" asked Malice. She could tell from their faces that they did not. It was a good job she wrote everything down. She opened her notebook and flicked to the page and read:

> This is more than just a business.
> It's a calling, don't you know.
> What seems rotten on the surface
> hides a danger way beneath.
> Sometimes it takes a witch's guile
> to protect against a thief.

"The witches are guarding something. People look at them and think they're rotten, when all the time they are guarding a danger much worse under the ground.

279

Something that they have to protect against thieves," said Malice. "They said it was a *calling*, so it could be like a quest or something?"

She didn't like to brag but she was feeling pretty good about herself right now. Any old fool could solve a problem with their fists but not everyone was good at solving problems with their brains.

"Like those knights who are supposed to protect the holy grail!" said Seth. "I watched it in an Indiana Jones movie!"

"Huh?" said Uncle Vex and Malice together. Topunders didn't really do telly.

"But what is it that they are protecting?" asked Uncle Vex.

"And why do the Grudges want it so badly?" asked Seth.

"And what does it have to do with my parents?" asked Malice. "There's only one thing for it, we need to visit to the Shipton witches again."

"I'm not emotionally ready to visit the emporium again yet," said Uncle Vex.

"We don't have to," said Malice brightly. "The shop is shut; we're going to pay them a home visit."

Malice grinned as Uncle Vex's face turned a pale grey.

28

HAVE YOU EVER HEARD OF THE MINOTAUR?

The Shipton witches lived in a flat behind the shop. Uncle Vex hailed them a hansom cab – a small carriage pulled by a horse – and paid the driver extra for a speedy journey. The bumping and rocking as they tore along the cobbled streets caused Antipathy-Rose to fall asleep and Uncle Vex to vomit out of the window. But they arrived in good time and were soon knocking on the witches' front door in an unlit alleyway at the back of the building.

The door creaked open and the sound of high-pitched cackling drifted out to them.

"What are they doing in there?" Uncle Vex was visibly quaking. "Maybe I should stay out here and keep watch."

Something black and sinuous slithered past them and out of sight down the alley.

"On second thoughts, let's go in and I'll keep watch … maybe from behind the locked bathroom door," he added, and pushed them into the flat.

They followed the sound of cackling and unintelligible chatter down a hallway lit by floating candles, which cast long shadows on the dark green walls, until they reached a door. Malice paused for a moment, wondering if there was any point in knocking when the witches clearly knew they were there, when she heard a voice that made her stomach flip in the best way.

"All's fair in love and poker, ladies!" it said.

Malice smiled and pushed open the door.

"Grandad!" she exclaimed. "What are you doing here?"

"Hello, duck!" Grandad grinned at her. "It's my Friday night poker game. I never miss an opportunity to play poker with these fine ladies." He waggled his eyebrows at each witch and Malice was surprised to see them blush and look coy in return.

The Shipton witches began to speak.

"The clues have brought you to our door, the answers now you seek."

"Sit down a while and rest your bones and listen while we speak."

Malice didn't really want to sit down a while; she wanted to find out what the witches were hiding and get this case wrapped up and her parents exonerated as soon as possible. But she knew better than to try and hurry the witches, it only made them go on longer. So, they sat. Grandad excused himself from the poker table and joined them on the surprisingly squishy sofas. Antipathy-Rose snored quietly on Malice's lap.

"Have you ever heard of the Minotaur?" asked Miasma.

Seth shot his hand up in the air. "Ooh, me! Pick me!"

Blight motioned for him to speak.

"The Minotaur was a beast in Greek mythology: half-man, half-bull, who was so dangerous he had to be kept in a specially built labyrinth below the city."

"Correct," said Pestilence.

"But if my Greek mythology serves me well, the Minotaur is dead – it was killed by Theseus," said Uncle Vex.

"Very good," said Miasma. "But he was just one beast. Over millennia, the labyrinth was used as a place to lose creatures who were too dangerous to be allowed to roam Underland. And certainly too dangerous to be allowed to escape Topside."

"So, the labyrinth is still in use?" Malice asked.

"No new creatures have been banished there for the last thousand years," said Blight. "But those still roaming the tunnels of the labyrinth pose a grave threat to the living, the dead and the living dead alike."

"You don't mean to say... You can't possibly... Surely it isn't..." Uncle Vex gulped.

"It most surely is," said Pestilence. "The only entrance left to the labyrinth lies beneath this building."

"We are sworn to protect it," added Miasma. "We are all that stands between death as we know it … and chaos."

"Our family has kept the entrance safe for thousands of years. And now it's our turn. No one but us has ever known what peril lies beneath," said Blight. "But somehow, the Grudges found out."

"But what is it they want?" Malice asked.

"Power!" said Pestilence. "Whoever sets the monsters free, holds dominion over them."

"And with control over the most terrifying creatures in history, they would have power over everything!"

Uncle Vex had pulled a fan from his jacket pocket and was fanning himself feverishly.

"But you said you wouldn't sell them the shop," said Malice.

"Do you think that will stop them?" asked Miasma, with a raised eyebrow. "This is only the beginning. They'll stop at nothing to get their hands on the labyrinth."

"Couldn't you tell the police?" asked Seth.

"The more who know the secret we hide, the more risk to the safety of both our worlds," said Blight. "We have only told you because you are directly involved."

"And if you hadn't fathomed the clues for yourselves, we wouldn't have told *you* either," added Pestilence.

Everyone was quiet for a few moments, absorbing the gravity of the situation. Malice stood up.

"I can stop them," she said.

All eyes fell on her.

"I know who framed my parents and how they did it. And I will make sure that your secret stays safe," she said to the witches.

"With respect, old girl, this case just got a lot bigger than your parents," said Uncle Vex.

"No, it didn't," Malice protested. "And if I can prove their innocence, I can stop the Grudges' evil plan at the same time."

Malice looked around her.

"Who's with me?" she asked.

"Me! Always!" said Seth, jumping up off the sofa.

"One hundred per cent," said Grandad.

Uncle Vex stood up, twirled his quiff and carefully placed his hat on his head.

"I love you as a niece and respect you as an intellect," said Uncle Vex. "Let's do this!" And then he added, "What are we actually doing?"

"We're going back to court," said Malice.

29

IT ALL STARTS WITH THE BACK OF MY TROUSERS!

The courthouse was more subdued this late at night and Judge Vulpine was extraordinarily grumpy at having been yanked out of bed by Blight. At Malice's request, the witches had sent invitations to the mayor, the Grudges and Chief Braggart. Ma and Pa stood in the dock wearing matching striped pyjamas and handcuffs. They smiled at her encouragingly. They looked tired.

Malice's hands were clammy with nerves, but she

knew she was right about this. Uncle Vex, Seth and Grandad watched from the gallery. Antipathy-Rose was curled up like a cat asleep on Grandad's lap.

"This had better be good!" bellowed Judge Vulpine and Malice flinched, almost dropping her notebook, but she recovered and shakily pulled herself up to her full height.

"I am here to prove my parents' innocence," she began.

"Get on with it then!" shouted a journalist from the seats at the back.

"I would like to call Animosity and Vendetta Grudge to the stand," Malice said, her voice sounding squeaky and small even to herself.

The Grudges blustered but did as they were asked.

"Please tell the court where you were at 7 p.m. last night," said Malice.

The Grudges smirked.

"We were in the King's Head pub having a business

meeting with the Shipton witches," said Animosity.

"Is this true?" the judge asked the witches.

All three witches nodded.

"It is, Your Honour," they chimed.

"So, at 7 p.m. you were at the pub, and therefore couldn't possibly have ghostnapped Mayor Dawdle."

"Correct!" said Vendetta. "Cast. Iron. Alibi."

"It would appear that way," Malice said, beginning to find her stride. "Unless 7 p.m. wasn't really 7 p.m!"

"Are you saying the mayor was mistaken about the time she was ghostnapped?" asked Judge Vulpine.

"Not exactly," said Malice.

"Then explain *exactly* what you *do* mean. Now!" the judge boomed.

The ferocity of the judge's voice almost caused Malice to stumble, but then she looked at her parents. Their hands were clasped together, and for the first time since that morning, she saw something like hope

in their eyes and it gave her the strength to go on.

And so she did.

Malice began by reading out the witches' riddle.

"When time is never on your side

    it's hard to spot the trick.

On its face, time ticks for Tardy,

    or does it go tock-tick?

Forwards, backwards, what a blunder,

    the hands of time are forced.

Reluctant rogue, poor shy Topunder,

    a quest to be endorsed.

A consultation taken with a

    side order of ruse,

Hides a wrong pinned on to rivals

    with indubitable clues.

It takes a cunning plan to be in

    two places at a time,

With witnesses to prove that you

were nowhere near the crime.
A lie is made more sturdy when
it's camouflaged in fact,
Dispute each truth, unpick the
proof, leave no alibi intact."

"The key to the whole thing, if you'll pardon the pun, is Mayor Dawdle's grandfather clock key," said Malice, "which was found in the glass clock face instead of where the mayor normally leaves it. Leading us to assume that someone had been in her house, tampering with her clock."

In spite of herself, she was having fun. Nothing made her tummy tingle like solving a tricky puzzle. She pointed to the first line.

> "When time is never on your side
> > it's hard to spot the trick.
> On its face, time ticks for Tardy,
> > or does it go tock-tick?"

"Mayor Dawdle is late for everything; she's well known for it. Which is why nobody raised the alarm at first when she didn't turn up for her breakfast meeting this morning. Then comes the next clue: *or does it go tock-tick?* It's backwards, everyone knows clocks tick-tock, not tock-tick."

Malice ran her fingers down to the next lines.

> "Forwards, backwards, what a blunder,
> > the hands of time are forced."

"The hands of the clock were literally being forced backwards to change the time."

"But surely even a ghost as perpetually late

as Tardy Dawdle would notice if her clock was suddenly slow?" Judge Vulpine challenged.

"Not if the clock was being turned back in small increments of, say, five minutes a day. Especially not with her terrible timekeeping. It's like the riddle said: when time is never on your side it's hard to spot the trick."

"And just who do you accuse of breaking into the mayor's home every day to change the time?"

Malice gulped.

"Maudlin Grudge, Your Honour," she said.

There was an affronted gasp from the Grudges. But Malice kept going. She read out another line from the witches' riddle:

"Reluctant rogue, poor shy Topunder,
a quest to be endorsed."

"The reluctant rogue was Maudlin Grudge. The MacNe'erdoowells saw Maudlin six mornings in a row when they were doing Spook-Chi in the garden of the Burke and Hare B&B. I asked them to send you a ghoulagram to confirm."

Judge Vulpine glared at an ashen-faced usher who handed her a piece of paper. The judge read the message from the MacNe'erdoowells and nodded.

"Proceed!" she said.

Malice cleared her throat. Maudlin looked even more glum than usual and she felt pretty terrible dropping him in it, but it was the truth after all. What else could she do?

"Six lots of five minutes would add up to half an hour in total. The Grudges needed the time to be turned back to give them an alibi." Malice read another few lines of the riddle.

"It takes a cunning plan to be
in two places at a time,
With witnesses to prove that you
were nowhere near the crime."

And then continued: "They arranged to meet the witches at 6.45 p.m. real time and left the pub half an hour later at 7.15 p.m. *real time* – which is fifteen minutes *after* the mayor believes she was taken – and then they ghostnapped the mayor at half-past seven, having already secured their alibi.

"A consultation taken with a
side order of ruse,
Hides a wrong pinned on to rivals
with indubitable clues."

"And your parents are the 'rivals' who've had the 'wrong pinned on to' them, I presume?" Judge Vulpine mused.

"Yes, Your Honour," said Malice and read out another line from the riddle.

"A lie is made more sturdy when
    it's camouflaged in fact."

The judge tented her fingers in front of her face.

"So, when Mayor Dawdle thought it was seven o'clock, it was in fact seven thirty," confirmed the judge.

"Yes," said Malice.

"And how did Mayor Dawdle not notice someone in her flat for six mornings in a row?"

"The mayor takes a run each morning," said Malice.

The mayor, sitting in the stalls nodded vigorously.

"The MacNe'erdoowells saw her leave each morning, followed by Maudlin arriving," Malice went on.

"This is all very interesting, but do you have any forensic evidence which places the Grudges at the scenes of the crime?" the judge asked in a bored voice.

Uncle Vex jumped up in the gallery and shouted, "Indeed we do, Your Honour! And it all starts with the back of my trousers!"

REMEMBER THE GRUDGE
CODE OF DISHONOUR

Uncle Vex and Seth ran down the stairs from the
gallery and came to stand next to Malice. Uncle
Vex looked delighted to be the centre of attention,
whereas Seth, not so much.

"This is outrageous!" screeched Vendetta, jumping
to her feet and causing fur from her moulting yeti
coat to flutter in the air. "I'll not stand for it!"

"Then sit!" said the judge with a quiet authority
that deflated Vendetta's bluster like a pin in a

whoopie cushion.

Vendetta sat. Her bottom lip jutted out in an exaggerated pout.

The judge addressed Malice, Seth and Uncle Vex.

"Let's get on with this. Please show the court the evidence which you believe puts the Grudges at the scenes of the crime."

Uncle Vex bowed low in the judge's direction.

"Seth, would you be so kind?"

Seth opened his rucksack and the two of them began to lay out envelopes across the evidence table in front of the judge.

"In both Mayor Dawdle's office and that of Tetchy-Sue Malign's, we found the same kinds of animal hair. This hair was also discovered on the sack used to cover the mayor's head during the ghostnap. Since neither the victim nor the accused owns any pets, we concluded that the animal hair must have transferred from the true perpetrators."

Uncle Vex used tweezers to extract the hair from the envelopes and showed it to the judge, who nodded.

"If I might be so bold?" he gestured to the judge's cloak with his tweezers and then picked off several hairs which had floated down on to it during Vendetta's outburst. Then, quick as a flash, before she had a chance to punch him, he leaped over to Vendetta Grudge and plucked several hairs from her coat.

"'Ere! You can't do that!" shouted Vendetta.

"Oh, but I have, dear lady." Uncle Vex smiled charmingly.

He crossed back to Judge Vulpine and dropped the hairs on to her desk.

"Would you mind comparing the hairs from Vendetta's coat with those from my evidence envelopes and your gown?" he asked politely.

Seth handed the judge a magnifying glass and the

judge studied the hairs. When she looked up, her face was steely. She addressed Vendetta Grudge.

"Yeti hair," she said coldly.

"Precisely," said Uncle Vex. "Yeti hair, moulted from Vendetta Grudge's coat as she ghost-handled Tardy Dawdle out of her office and into the oubliette at Malignant House."

"It's a stitch up!" screeched Vendetta, jumping to her feet. "Tell 'em, Animosity! Tell 'em!"

Animosity, who had been scowling particularly hard for the last few minutes, rubbed his beard thoughtfully and then said, "I had nothing to do with it. I am as surprised as you are, Your Honour." He turned and grimaced at his wife. "Sorry, my venomous viper, you're on your own."

"What??" Vendetta screamed. "Oh no you don't! If I'm going down, you're going down with me!" Spittle flew from her mouth as she spat the words. "You traitorous fiend!"

Animosity shrugged.

"She must have cooked up the scheme with Maudlin. I had nothing to do with it." He got up to leave, but Chief Braggart barred his exit.

"You can't pin this on me!" Animosity snarled. "You can't even place me at the scene of the crime; you've got nothing!"

"That's not quite true," said Uncle Vex, picking up another envelope.

Animosity was firmly encouraged to sit back down and held there by Chief Braggart's meaty hands pressing down on his shoulders.

"The only possible way that the Grudges could have got into and out of Malignant House without being seen is if they used the portal to Underland in Tetchy-Sue's office," Uncle Vex continued. "Unfortunately, speedy though it may be, it tends to leave its mark."

Uncle Vex turned around, bent over and lifted

his suit jacket to show the flecks of paint which had transferred from the tea tray at the portal on to his suit trousers. When everyone had taken a good look, he straightened back up and took a pocket mirror from his suit, re-smoothing his hair and straightening his tie.

"Malice, Seth, would you mind?" Uncle Vex asked, gesturing to the envelopes.

They picked one envelope each, showed the labels pertaining to where the evidence was discovered to the judge, and tipped the contents out on to the desk.

"Paint flecks," said Uncle Vex. "Pustule Green Number Five found in Mayor Dawdle's study and in Tetchy-Sue's home office. The very paint used for the leaves on the tea tray."

"So?" leered Animosity. "That don't mean nothing!"

"*Au contraire.*" Uncle Vex met his leer with a smile. "Chief Constable Braggart, would you mind helping Mr Grudge to stand?"

Chief Braggart pulled Animosity roughly to his feet.

"And if you could just turn him around," Uncle Vex continued.

Animosity was turned. Uncle Vex stepped lightly over and lifted Animosity's leather jacket. The little crowd gasped. Vendetta cackled gleefully. For there on the back of Animosity's trousers, were paint flakes that matched the ones found at the scenes of the crime, transferred from the tea tray in the private portal.

"Your Honour, it would take only a little research to discover that Pustule Green Number Five was discontinued in the late nineteenth century, around the same time that private portals were closed. The paint on mine and Animosity's trousers could only have come from the Malign's private portal."

Judge Vulpine looked intrigued.

"Do you have anything to say?" the judge asked Animosity.

Animosity looked blown up like a puffer fish.

"Plenty!" he began, but he was cut short when Maudlin stood up and raised his hand.

"Yes, young man?" the judge said. "Do you wish to speak?"

"Keep it shut, Maudlin!" growled Animosity.

"Remember the Grudge code of dishonour," hissed Vendetta. "Say nuffink, pass the buck, throw some shade and sling the muck."

Maudlin looked at his parents and then at Malice and then at the floor. He looked hopelessly lost and, despite it all, Malice's heart went out to him. She poured a glass of water and took it over to him.

"If you don't want to talk,

you don't have to," she said quietly.

Maudlin took a long drink. When he'd finished, he wiped his mouth and gave her a wan smile.

"Thank you," he said. He turned and addressed the judge. "It's all true. I crept into the mayor's office and turned her grandfather clock back by five minutes each morning. I didn't know at the time what the plan was. I just thought that my morning mischief was to make the mayor late for her meetings. I wanted to make my parents proud. I'm a disappointment to them, you see, with my bathing and reading."

Malice couldn't believe her ears; *bathing and reading*? The Grudges were always banging on about how brilliantly mischievous their Maudlin was. Malice had always felt like a disappointment to her poor parents while they listened to the fantastic tales of Maudlin's mischief. Could it all have been a front to cover up Maudlin's lack of mischief ability?

Maudlin was still speaking.

"I was supposed to go back into the mayor's flat this morning and turn the clock back to the right time, but I overslept. And then when I went back later, Malice was there with her friend Seth and her family. I should have said something sooner. I should have come forward." Maudlin looked from Judge Vulpine to Malice. "But they're my parents," he said pleadingly.

"I understand," said Malice. And she did – she really did. It wasn't easy when you didn't feel like you fit with your family. The difference was that over time Ma and Pa had learned to accept Malice's strange ways and she'd accepted theirs. She wasn't sure Maudlin had been quite so lucky with his parents.

"I'm sorry, Malice," said Maudlin. "I'm sorry your parents are in this mess because of me. I'm a coward as well as a rubbish mischief-maker."

"Well, it isn't only down to you," said Malice. "But apology accepted." She gave Maudlin what she hoped

was her friendliest smile.

"There is nothing whatsoever cowardly in what you've just done," said Uncle Vex.

He stepped forward and held out his hand. Maudlin tentatively shook it. Then Seth did the same.

The air was suddenly filled with a screech of rage that caused the living and the dead to cover their ears. It came from Vendetta Grudge. She looked like a wild thing; her eyes blazed, her brown teeth bared as she snarled and fought against her captors.

"It's all your fault, Malice Morbid Malign!" she spat at Malice. "You did this! It was all going to be so perfect. Getting the Maligns out of the way was just the first part of the plan. We'd have gone after each and every Topunder family and made them bow in our presence. Animosity and me were gonna rule Underland and Topside; we were gonna rule it all by fear! You would all be our minions!"

Fizzy frogs' legs! thought Malice, at this rate

Vendetta was going to give the witches secret away. She'd managed to keep their motive for framing her parents out of the equation, but if Vendetta kept spouting off like this it would be game over!

Luckily, Uncle Vex was on hand for a charm offensive.

"Your Honour, it seems clear to me that poor Mrs Grudge is having some sort of delusional meltdown. She's clearly talking nonsense. She is quite possibly a megalomaniac."

Judge Vulpine nodded sagely.

"I do believe you are right."

31

A MOST
REMARKABLE MALIGN

A silence broke over the courtroom, which felt heavy and claustrophobic, as all eyes turned to the judge. Vendetta had exhausted herself and sat limply half on and half off her chair. Animosity stared straight ahead, a look of resignation on his dirty face. Judge Vulpine held the bridge of her nose with her thumb and forefinger. She looked deep in thought. After a long moment, she spoke.

"Chief Constable Braggart, kindly take Mr and

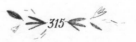

Mrs Grudge into custody and free Pugnacious and Tetchy-Sue Malign immediately. They are clearly innocent of this particular crime."

The courtroom erupted into noise. Malice and Seth did jump hugs while shouting "Woo-hoo!"

Animosity and Vendetta cursed loudly at each other, at the judge, at the chief constable and especially at the three detectives.

"You'll get yours!" Vendetta screeched.

"You'll get yours first!" Malice retorted, poking her tongue out. It was most unlike Malice to retaliate but really, when someone has tried to frame your parents and take over the world, a little bit of tongue-poking is probably in order.

Police officers spilled into the courtroom to secure the prisoners and Chief Braggart removed Ma and Pa's handcuffs whilst making blustery apologies under his breath. As soon as they were uncuffed, Malice ran to them.

"My girl!" cried Ma, hugging Malice tightly. "You did it."

As Ma released her, Pa pulled her into another hug.

"You clever little maggot," he sniffed. "I could not be more proud. You might be a bit mediocre in the mischief department, but you're whip-smart and wily and I'm coming to realize that's just as important as being a miscreant."

Malice felt explosively happy. Not so long ago her Pa would have sooner cleaned behind his ears than be proud to have a clever daughter.

"I had a lot of assistance," said Malice when her parents had finished swapping her back and forth between them.

"That you did," Ma agreed. "Vexatious, though I cannot condone your excessive use of lavender soap, and your do-gooding sickens me, I am grateful for all your hard work. And for keeping my girls safe."

Malice's eyes were wide with wonder. This was unprecedented.

"My brother!" exclaimed Pa, lip wobbling with emotion. "I missed you so, all those years we were apart. I missed you so. I'm glad you're on my team." Pa squeezed Uncle Vex, nestling his head into Vex's suit jacket, because Pa was very short and Uncle Vex was rather tall. "You stink though, bro," he added. "Maybe try and dirty yourself up a bit?"

Uncle Vex smiled.

"In the interests of compromise, I could maybe

think about only bathing every other day?" he suggested.

"It's a start." Pa smiled, patting his younger brother's back.

Ma looked over at Seth. He still had moss behind his ears and drain gloop in his matted hair. He looked like he'd taken a swim in a sewer, and he didn't smell much better.

"Well, aren't you a sight for sore eyes," said Ma affectionately. "I can whiff your stink from here. Seth, you know I have been unsure about your Topsider ways and your suspicious cleanliness, but today you've done yourself proud. If Malice must have a friend, I'm glad it's you."

Malice was astonished. This night was turning out to be even weirder than the day they'd just had.

Grandad came over with Antipathy-Rose, who had woken up at hearing her parents' voices, and the jollifications began anew. Antipathy-Rose screeched

delightedly, "Ma. Pa. Ma. Pa. Bite!" as she was passed around the family and hugged and squeezed by all.

The Grudges were taken down to the Underland dungeons, hissing and spitting at everyone as they went. As the doors swung closed behind them, Malice turned and caught sight of Maudlin, sitting all alone, staring at the space left behind by his parents.

"Oh no!" she exclaimed. "What's going to happen to Maudlin?"

Seth looked over at the sullen boy in the corner.

"Cripes!" said Seth. "I'd forgotten about him. He must feel pretty rubbish right now."

"And lonely," Malice agreed.

Uncle Vex looked thoughtful.

"And probably scared," he reasoned. "This is a pretty pickle. What to do?"

"We can't leave him by himself." Malice felt desperate for Maudlin, despite it all.

"You really are a most remarkable Malign."

Uncle Vex smiled. "That boy has just confessed to contributing to the wrongful arrest of your parents and you're worried about his welfare."

Malice considered this. But whichever way she looked at it, she couldn't hate Maudlin for what he had done. After all, hadn't he been going along with mischief to please his parents, just as she herself had done countless times before?

"It doesn't matter," she said. "We have to help him. His was miscalculated mischief, misguided and misinformed, but I don't believe it was malicious! I know what it feels like to want to fit in."

Seth rubbed her arm.

"Remember what my dads call us?" he smiled. "Two square pegs in a round-hole world! Maybe Maudlin is another square peg."

Uncle Vex chewed his lip thoughtfully.

"You're quite right, you two. Wise beyond your ears, as usual."

"Don't you mean, *years*?" asked Seth.

"I know what I mean, young man."

"What will happen to him?" Malice asked.

"That's down to the judge," said Uncle Vex, "and whether or not he has other family who can take him in."

Pa called Uncle Vex back over to where the grown-ups were talking. Malice looked at Seth.

"I think he could do with a friend or two," said Malice.

"I was just thinking that!" Seth replied.

Malice could see Maudlin stiffen in his chair as they walked towards him. He managed to look everywhere but at Malice and Seth.

"Hey, Maudlin," said Malice quietly. Suddenly she didn't know what to say. "How are you doing?"

"We're sorry about your parents," added Seth. "That's really rough.

Maudlin looked at them for the first time. He was

frowning; he looked confused and apprehensive.

"Is this a trick?" he asked, hesitatingly.

"No," said Malice.

"We mean it," said Seth. "Honest."

"You mean … you mean, you don't hate me?" he asked.

"Nah," said Malice. "Whose got time for hate?"

"My dad says hate is a very destructive emotion," added Seth.

Malice couldn't be sure, but she thought she detected the ghost of a smile on Maudlin's face – but then it vanished just as quickly.

"I don't know what to do," he said. "I don't belong anywhere."

"I'll tell you where you belong!" snapped Ma.

Everybody turned to see Ma pursing her lips, her hands resting on her bony hips. *Oh dear!* Malice chewed her lip and Seth pulled an *eek!* face. It felt like the whole room was holding its breath … even

the ghosts!

"You belong right here with us," said Ma, smiling to reveal a row of gold teeth. "Vex said you needed somewhere to stay. We've squared it with the judge. If you want us, we'll be your family. We ain't perfect, but we've got love."

"Ma's right," agreed Pa. "We've never done books, we're not fans of education and yet, despite our best efforts, we've learned a thing or two."

Ma took Pa's hand.

"We're a right motley bunch in this family," said Ma. "Do-gooders and mischief-makers, all rubbing along together. It ought not to work but somehow it does. Somehow our differences make our family stronger. And I'll tell you something else," she said, holding her arms out to Maudlin. "There's always room for one more."

32

THE BAT DROPPINGS ARE BARELY COVERING THE RUG

It was the morning of the All Hallows' Haunt and Ma was in a tizz.

"It'll never be ready!" she wailed. "We lost a whole day's prep time languishing in a blooming jail cell."

"Calm down, my precious warthog," Pa soothed. "We'll all pitch in and get it done. Won't we?" He looked at Malice, Seth and Maudlin.

They were sitting at the kitchen table eating breakfast. Seth had been allowed to stay for another

sleepover, and Maudlin was getting used to living with the Maligns. Malice and Maudlin were tucking into their frosted beetle cereal with enthusiasm. Seth was less enthusiastic.

"'Course, Ma," said Malice, picking a beetle leg out of her teeth. "Whatever you need, we're here to h—" she stopped herself just in time.

Pa shook his head, smiling.

"Go on then," he said. "With a house full of do-gooders, I suppose I'd better get used to it."

Malice grinned.

"We're here to help!" she said.

Pa still winced at the word "help", but at least it no longer caused him to feel faint.

"I've hardly had time to do a deep stink-up in the guest bedrooms. The dust is only two centimetres thick in the drawing room and the bat droppings in the sitting rooms are barely covering the rugs. Whatever are our guests going to think of me?" Ma

was choking back sobs now. "And the ballroom!" she sniffed. "A crow got in through the window and ate the spiders; the webs are pitiful, not a decent haunted house cobweb among them."

"Um, I might have an idea," ventured Seth. "Of how we could very quickly trash the place up a bit."

Ma looked at him.

"Really?" she sounded hopeful as she wiped her nose all the way from her wrist to her elbow.

Seth nodded.

"I'll have to call my dads, though."

"Whatever you need, boy," said Pa. "The telephone's in the hall."

The telephone was one of the old-fashioned candlestick phones; sleek and black with a separate handle on a hook and a dial that required multiple turnings to call the number you required. Malice showed Seth how to use it and they waited for one of his dads to answer.

Half an hour later, the doorbell rang and Seth's dads, Bill and Pete, were standing on the doorstep dressed in overalls. Pete was holding a leaf blower and surrounded by two full garden sacks and a garden waste wheelie bin, while Bill held the Hoover and two further carrier bags stuffed to bursting.

"Hello, you two!" said Pete. "Did you have a good sleepover?"

"It was brilliant, dad. I had four ghosts in my room and Bernhard the skeleton let me read his comics."

Seth's dads looked from Seth to Malice, perplexed. Malice just smiled and invited them in.

"I managed to get the neighbours to empty their Hoovers as well," said Bill.

"This really is the weirdest request you have ever made of us, Seth," added Pete.

The two men looked around the grand, old,

dilapidated entrance hall. They'd never been inside Malignant House before.

"This is magnificent!" exclaimed Pete.

"Your parents sure know how to dress a house up for Halloween," added Bill.

Malice smiled; they didn't need to know that this was how her house always looked.

"So, what are we doing?" asked Bill.

"If you could empty the dust from the hoover into the bedrooms upstairs," Malice began. "Some of the guests haven't been here in over a hundred and fifty years, Ma wants to impress them."

"That long, huh?" Bill smirked, nudging Pete, who gave him a wink.

"Um, yes," Malice replied. "And then if you could chuck the garden waste in and around the general ballroom area and then blow it about a bit with the leaf blower, just to get it evenly distributed. And anything left over can be thrown about in the drawing

331

and sitting rooms, if that's OK?"

Bill and Pete shared a look, then shrugged their shoulders and set to work, directed by Seth.

By the time they were done, the house was magnificently ghastly. The guest rooms were particularly gruesome. Malice had managed to bulk out the cobwebs with Hoover dust and the autumn leaves which covered the floors gave the ballroom and corridors a marvellously abandoned eerie feeling of decay. Maudlin had sneaked about Felicity Square and emptied the food recycling bins into a sack. Then he spread the putrefying food over the fireplaces and hung old banana skins from the chandeliers.

When Ma came in with the canapés to give them time to warm up and get germy, she almost dropped where she stood.

"Oh my gawd!" she exclaimed. "It's beautiful!"

Malice introduced Pete and Bill to her parents, and it went surprisingly well.

"We're not normally keen on Topsiders," Ma said to Bill. "But we've made an exception for Seth. He can be a bit too clean at times, but he tries, and you can't ask for more than that, can you?"

"Er, no, I guess not," Bill replied, bemused.

Malice found Pa showing Pete the bog pond in the garden.

"I'm telling you, Pete, after a hard day's mischief you can't beat a good long soak in the bog and a fox-poo facemask. That's how I keep looking so young!" said Pa.

Pete nodded uncertainly and said he'd give Pa's invitation to join him and Ma for a spa evening some thought.

When it was time for Seth and his dads to leave so that Seth could change ready for the ball, Ma surprised everyone by inviting Bill and Pete as well.

"In for a penny, in for a pound," said Ma when Malice quizzed her on it later. "I've decided to invite

the Topunder families we snubbed before as well. The Pinchers, Brigands, Racketeers and Savages. And, of course, the MacNe'erdoowells; after all, they helped to get us out of prison."

"That's true," agreed Malice. "Their observations helped me work out how the Grudges had done it."

"And you know," Ma said thoughtfully, "I think carrying around those spiteful feelings all the time was starting to give me an ulcer."

I WOULDN'T HAVE 'EM
ANY OTHER WAY

As the clock struck midnight, the guests began to arrive. Felicity Square was awash with Topunder family vehicles. Horses and carriages, rusty old Mercedes, beaten-up Beamers, a couple of sleighs pulled by huskies, and twenty-five Harley Davidson motorbikes (the Stonehenge Stenches' preferred mode of transportation).

The ghosts, ghouls, witches and vampires arrived either via the portal in Ma's office, or they simply

drifted up through the floorboards in their finery. It was the most exciting thing that had ever happened at Malignant House, and Malice was beside herself with glee.

Seth, who was wearing a blue velvet doublet, matching hose and a strikingly large ruff, leaned in to whisper into Malice's ear.

"My dads think this is brilliant! They're trying to work out where the projectors are; they think the ghosts are video footage!" he sniggered.

"Probably best to let them carry on thinking it," Malice giggled. "They might freak out if they know they're all real!"

"I don't know what they're going to make of the zombie dance troupe!"

Uncle Vex was wearing a particularly sharp suit and, to Malice's surprise, Maudlin was wearing one identical.

"Had Madame Suture knock him one up," said Uncle Vex.

Maudlin actually looked happy. Malice had never seen him look happy; it would take her a while to get used to it, but she liked it.

"I asked him if he was interested in solving crime," said Uncle Vex. "But sadly not."

Maudlin shook his head.

"Nah, I like Art: painting and stuff," said Maudlin.

Pa came over, wearing a suit which was at least five sizes too small. His beard was extra greasy for the occasion.

"Painting, you say?" Pa grinned mischievously. "We've never had a painter in the family before. I feel

a new avenue in forgery opening up! Let's me and you take a little trip to the National Gallery in the week, yeah?" He rubbed his hands together and Malice rolled her eyes and laughed.

There was a clinking sound, and everyone turned to the stage at the far end of the ballroom where Ma was tapping a jackdaw skull against her glass. Tonight she was wearing a swishy black ballgown of tattered lace and the tiara of diamond skulls with ruby eyes. Her skin looked deathly pale and her blood-red lips matched the rubies in her tiara.

"Isn't she exquisite?!" Pa sighed, dabbing at a tear on his cheek with a snotty handkerchief. Malice couldn't agree more.

"Ahem," Ma cleared her throat and three hundred guests, living, dead and the living dead, fell quiet. "I don't normally say this kind of stuff and you may never hear me use these words again after tonight but thank you."

Gasps came from all around the ballroom at this.

"Thank you all for coming," Ma continued. "And a special thank you to my daughter Malice, her friend Seth and my brother-in-law Vexatious, for working tirelessly to get me and Pa out of jail. We don't always see eye to eye, and I'll never understand the allure of a scented bath bomb or even a bath come to that, but they're family. I love 'em all, and I wouldn't 'ave 'em any other way." Ma raised her glass. "To family!" she shouted. "In whatever forms they take!"

Cheers erupted around the ballroom. Seth was squashed in a dad-hug-sandwich. Antipathy-Rose toddled over to Malice with her arms outstretched.

Malice picked her little sister up.

"Are you enjoying the party?" Malice asked, and her sister nodded. She was gnawing on something metal. "Is that a belt buckle?"

Antipathy-Rose grinned, showing a double row of pointed teeth. A few feet away a ghost shrieked as his trousers fell down around his ankles.

"My belt!" he shouted. "It's been sheared right through!"

Malice and Antipathy-Rose fell into giggles.

"'Ello, duck," said Grandad, floating up beside her. "Look who I've found!"

"Nana!" Malice squealed in delight.

Nana Rascally wrapped her ghostly arms around Malice and Antipathy-Rose.

"I'll be here for a few days," said Nana. "The coven is looking after the hotel for me, so we can have a proper catch up. I want to hear all about your mystery solving adventures."

"Speaking of which," said Grandad, "I've just had a ghoulagram from one of the grandads down at the club. Seems there's been a spate of grave robberies over at Highgate cemetery. They're stealing teeth! He wondered if the Underland Investigators would be interested in taking the case."

"Sounds right up our street," said Malice. "Thanks for the tip-off."

"My clever granddaughter," smiled Grandad. "You make me proud every day."

Malice felt the warmth of his words flow through her. Nana put her arms out to take Antipathy-Rose. She couldn't actually hold her, but she cast a spell so that the toddler could levitate beside her.

"Me and your grandad will watch this little

ankle-biter, so you can enjoy the ball," said Nana. "We'll catch up later." She gave Malice's cheek a ghosty squeeze and floated off with Grandad and Antipathy-Rose.

Back on the stage, Mayor Dawdle had begun to speak.

"I had a speech all ready for this evening. But as you know, I was ghostnapped recently. And so I'd like to take a moment to thank Malice, Seth and Vexatious Malign, Private Underland Investigators, for working tirelessly to crack the case. And Antipathy-Rose Malign for assisting them with her excellent gnashers. Were it not for them, I would still be napped and trapped in an oubliette. I hope we've all learned something from this, and that this All Hallows' Haunt is the start of new alliances and excellent mischief for the year to come. Without further ado, I declare this All Hallows' Haunt has begun!"

There was thunderous applause at this.

The orchestra struck up and the dancing began. Mordacious sat on Truculent's lap with her arms around his neck as he wheeled his chair back and forth to the music. Seth's dads expertly waltzed between couples swaying on the dance floor, and Ma and Pa danced a surprisingly passionate tango. Mayor Dawdle and Stinky Pincher made a fine-looking pair, dresses swirling as they spun cheek-to-cheek, while Judge Vulpine stood beside the piano, deep in conversation with Gaseous Racketeer. Nana Rascally and Grandad danced the foxtrot, and Antipathy-Rose floated along beside them on Nana's broomstick. Maudlin was being given a tour of the paintings, which hung all over the house, by the ghosts of Frida Kahlo and Leonardo Da Vinci and it seemed like now he'd learned how to smile, he would never stop.

34

THE BEST HALLOWEEN EVER!

Malice followed Uncle Vex's dreamy gaze across the ballroom to where Belladonna was sipping a glass of pumpkin wine. She politely declined an offer to dance from a tall, dark vampire, before casting a fleeting look towards Uncle Vex. Tonight, she looked more beguiling than even the most glamorous Hollywood movie star.

"Ask her to dance!" urged Malice.

"Oh, I couldn't possibly. I mean, I'd like to, of course, anyone with eyes in their head can see she's

a vision of loveliness; fascinating brain too, really exquisitely cunning ... but what if she says no?"

"But what if she says yes?" Malice encouraged.

"If you don't ask, you'll always be wondering," added Seth.

Uncle Vex nodded.

"You're right, of course. Sage advice, as always. Thanks chaps, wish me luck!"

He gave his quiff one final twizzle, straightened his jacket and set off across the dance floor, deftly avoiding the couples twirling all around him. Malice and Seth watched from the other side of the room as Uncle Vex and Belladonna made awkward small talk, clearly both wanting to dance but too shy or stubborn to make the first move.

"Get on with it!" sighed Seth in exasperation.

"So annoying!" Malice agreed.

"Maybe they need a little push," came a voice beside them.

They turned to see the Shipton witches twiddling their wands as they too watched Uncle Vex and Belladonna.

"What did you have in mind?" Malice asked.

"A little spell to loosen their limbs."

"To rectify their nervous whims."

"And give love wings like cherubim."

Seth and Malice looked at one another.

"What do you think?" asked Malice.

"Couldn't hurt, could it?" Seth replied.

"OK," said Malice to the witches. "But nothing fancy, just get them on the dance floor."

Blight, Pestilence and Miasma grinned and raised their wands.

"A little shove from Loki and a tap of Cupid's bow,

To help a nervous Topunder become a ghostie's beau.

Get them on the dance floor and make it happen fast,

A love spark on All Hallows' is a love that's sure to last."

The ends of their wands crackled, and Malice and Seth watched as the air shimmered around Uncle Vex and Belladonna. Suddenly, behind the pair, a portrait fell off the wall and banged hard down on to a table. The candelabra on the table wobbled, dislodging a single candle which rolled along the table, still lit, and came to rest beside an ornamental cannon. The flame set light to the fuse, which burned down, fizzing and popping like a sparkler. The sparkle caught Uncle Vex's eye and, quick as a flash, he grabbed Belladonna in his arms and spun her out of the line of fire. The

cannonball shot through the air and lodged in the wall behind Malice and Seth, punching a hole right through a portrait of Maniacal Malign's face.

In his haste to save Belladonna, Uncle Vex had unwittingly twirled her right on to the dance floor. And now there they stood, arms still wrapped around one another. The orchestra began to play "The Danse Macabre" and Uncle Vex and Belladonna, as though moved by magic, began to dance.

"Now *that* was cool!" said Seth.

Malice laughed.

"Fancy a boogie, bestie?" she asked.

"I thought you'd never ask." Seth grinned.

And the two friends hit the dance floor – Malice doing the monster mash and Seth doing the robot, surrounded by ghosts and ghouls and good friends. It was the best All Hallows' Haunt ever!

NAME: Malice Morbid Malign

AGE: 11 $^3/_4$

PROFESSION: Mischief-Maker
& Amateur Detective.

LIKES: Reading, Bathing, Puzzles.

DISLIKES: Malevolent Mischief, Messy
Bedrooms, Not Helping.

INTERESTING FACT: Malice discovered she
could talk to night creatures when she fell into
one of the sinking-bogs in the Malignant House
grounds, aged 4, and was rescued by two barn
owls and a fox named Darwin, who answered her
cries for help. Once a month she hosts a moonlit
supper-club for the night animals in the old
icehouse near the mausoleum.

NAME: Seth Indiana Pinkerton

AGE: 11 1/4

PROFESSION: Paperboy & Amateur Detective.

LIKES: Skeletons, Cycling, Weirdness.

DISLIKES: Meanness, Ordinary, Bedtime.

INTERESTING FACT: Seth shares the same surname as Allan Pinkerton, the founder of Pinkerton's National Detective Agency in America in 1850 who hired the first ever female detective : Kate Warne.

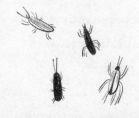

NAME: Tardy Swift Dawdle

AGE: 275

PROFESSION: Mayor of Underland

LIKES: Reading romance novels. Fire juggling.
Speed skating (she is the fastest speed skater in
Underland, but her perpetual lateness means that
she always misses the start of the race.)

DISLIKES: Unfairness. Milky tea. Timers.

INTERESTING FACT: Before Tardy became
Mayor, she was a librarian. She is a great friend
of Lewis Carroll — author of *Alice in Wonderland* —
who himself worked as a librarian when he lived
Topside. Tardy adores libraries because they give
everyone a fair chance to read books regardless of
how much money they have.

After sharing a dance at the All Hallows' Haunt, Uncle Vex finally plucked up the courage to ask Belladonna out on a date. They began the evening with tickets to see the famous Shakespeare play, *A Midwinter Night's Terror* at the Golem Theatre. From there they had a table booked at Nosferatu's restaurant where they enjoyed classic dishes of Ghoulash and Devilled Eggs. And they rounded the evening off with a romantic walk along Bone River beneath the glow-worm sky. The river glittered as they skimmed skulls across the water to see who could get the most cranium bounces. And when they'd run out of skulls, they bought boxes of entrails from one of the huts along the south bank and fed them to the crocodilians that swim in the murky depths. It was a perfect evening and hopefully the first of many; keep your phalanges crossed!

When Blight, Miasma and Pestilence heard that I was writing some extra pages, they immediately wanted to be involved. They have very kindly offered us their advice for creating the perfect All Hallows' Haunt.

Consider first the tastebuds of the monsters at your
*   feast,*
Is their pleasure gently rotted veg or putrid spit-roast
*   beast?*
Carve your jack-o-lanterns scary, cut your paper
*   chain skulls grim.*
Strings of popcorn make good nibbles, as does crispy
*   zombie skin.*
As the candles flicker gently and the logs pop in the
*   hearth,*
Let the banshees scare your guests to death, it's sure
*   to be a laugh.*

Strew your cobwebs with abandon, hang your
  pumpkin lights with zeal,
Fill a punch bowl with some witches' brew and a
  toothy conger eel.
Play spooky games like 'Tag, you're dead!' and bob for
  rotten fruit,
Hide and seek in graveyards is dead cert to be a hoot.
May your cauldron never boil dry, may your
  mischief light burn bright,
Happy Halloween to one and all, don't let the dead-
  bugs bite!

THE ALL HALLOWS' HAUNT

No one knows exactly when Underlanders and Topunders first came together to celebrate the All Hallows' Haunt. Although the first human written record is 200 BC, the Underland records go back much further. It is understood that it's been happening in one form or another for as long as there have been people alive and dead.

In the archives at the Witches' Library, there is an extract which describes witches, warlocks and Topunders using a mixture of magic and brute force to arrange a huge stone circle on a hill in the county we now call Wiltshire. This is of course Stonehenge. They then draped an enormous blanket of sewn-together animal skins over the whole structure to make a giant marquee in which they held that year's All Hallows' Haunt. It is said that the guests consumed a staggering six spit roast woolly mammoths that night.

For centuries, historians have tried to fathom the meaning of Stonehenge; it is one of the world's greatest mysteries. I wonder if they'd be disappointed to discover that it was basically just a massive party tent?

THE UNDERLAND INVESTIGATORS

Before I go, I thought I'd just catch you up on what the Underland Investigators have been up to since the All Hallows' Haunt.

It's been all go for Malice, Seth and Uncle Vex. They solved the Highgate Cemetery Tooth Heist — in which teeth were being removed from skeletons in their coffins — after a dizzying high speed chase through the graveyard and setting traps below the catacombs to catch the culprit.

Next came the Case of the Howling Bride: reports of a ghost in a wedding dress terrorizing the occupants of Lewisham. It turned out she'd accidentally got locked in the suitcase of a gentleman travelling from Romania to London. I am pleased to report that the investigators were able to reunite the bride with her somewhat bemused groom, who had been waiting for her in a haunted chapel in Transylvania.

Their latest case is most perplexing. A ghost in a tuxedo, calling himself the Enigmatic Enigma, has been charming the ladies of Underland out of their most prized pilfered possessions. It seems he has spread his troublesome ways Topside, as not only have Mordacious and Ma fallen victim to his charisma, but the BBC has just announced he has swindled the Queen of England. MI5 have contacted Malice, Seth and Uncle Vex for their help and the three Underland investigators are now on the case.

Acknowledgements

I have had the best time writing books about Malice.
I have enjoyed every single moment, from writing the
first few lines to editing the finished manuscripts. I will
be forever grateful for having the chance to see Malice's
adventures become books.

It takes a whole lot of creative, talented people to get a
story from first draft to a finished book; my name might
be on the cover but that is only the tip of the iceberg. And
that means that I have a lot of people to thank.

Malice's adventures began as my dissertation at
Canterbury Christ Church University where I studied as
a mature student. Thank you, Emily Guille-Marrett, for
being a brilliant lecturer and personal tutor, and for your
boundless enthusiasm and support.

Thank you, lovely Chloe *Scallywag* Seagar, my agent at the
marvellous Madeleine Milburn Literary Agency, for being
bouncy and excited about Malice from the very first draft.
Thank you for believing in me and working so hard to find
Malice and I a publishing home.

What can I say about the team at Scholastic? It has been
dreamy working with you. To my brilliant Editor, Yasmin
misbehaviour Morrissey, thank you for being as excited
about Malice's adventures as I am and for throwing
yourself fully into the Underland spirit! We first met when

covid was just a whisper on the wind ... we had no idea! Since then, there's been a global pandemic, lockdowns and you've had a gorgeous baby, and here we are on our final Malice journey together (sobs). Thank you, Yas, you are wonderful.

My thanks go to Sophie Cashell (Commissioning Editor) for taking me through the first drafts of Ghost Games. Your notes and advice helped me to shape my wild imaginings; this book is all the better for your input.

Thank you, Sarah Dutton, for being a brilliant Managing Editor. I have so enjoyed working with you, I feel like you really get me! Thank you for your keenness to let me try out an idea, no matter how bananas it might seem. Thanks too to Catherine Liney — Editorial Assistant and Kathy Webb — Copyeditor for all your hard work.

My thanks go to Andrew Biscomb, Art Director and Rachel Lawston for the gorgeous cover designs and details throughout the book that make every page a delight, you are so appreciated.

Lauren Fortune — Publisher, Catherine Bell — MD and Georgina Russell — Production Manager, I want to thank you for all your hard work to make this book happen!

Thank you, Harriet Dunlea — Publicist and Kiran Khanom — Publicity Assistant for being super lovely and virtually holding my hand during events. I am such a nervous-nelly, I literally couldn't do it without you!

When Yasmin told me she was going to ask Hannah Peck to illustrate the *Malice* series, I couldn't believe it and I hoped beyond hope that Hannah would agree. She did. Thank you, Hannah, for bringing my stories to life with your gloriously gothic, hilarious, sometimes terrifying illustrations. Every time I send you my character descriptions, I cannot wait to see what you will come up with and every time you blow my mind. You are such a talent and I feel grateful and humbled that you agreed to work with me.

To Harriett Evans at The Book Den in Hythe, thank you for your support, for championing Malice's adventures and for letting me launch my books in your beautiful book shop. You are a wonderful bookseller and your love for children's books shines out of you!

Thank you to my family and friends for being bananas and full of merry mischief, I love you all. And to Franchesca, who dressed up as Malice for World Book Day — you know who you are — you made my year, thank you!

And finally, thank you dear reader for taking Malice's journey with me. I hope you have enjoyed this book. Whether you like a scented bath bomb as Malice does, or you're a fan of keeping earwigs behind your ears, be sure to keep reading books because they are the key to all the magic in the universe.

Love, Jenni xxx

NAME: Jenni Louise Jennings

UNDERLAND NAME: Viper Deathstalker

AGE: 48

PROFESSION: Author of *Malice in Underland*, *A Trick of Time*, *Ghost Games* & *Merry Kissmas to You!*

LIKES: Reading. Chocolate. Walking by the sea. Spooky movies. Daydreaming. Kindness.

DISLIKES: Goat's cheese. Sticky fingers. Meanness. Bullies. Dog poo on my shoes.

INTERESTING FACT: When I was a young girl my favourite book was *The Worst Witch* by Jill Murphy. I desperately wanted to be a witch like my heroine Mildred Hubble. On the way home from my grandma's house, we used to pass a grand old building on a hill with crenellated towers. I was certain it was a Witches' Academy and would beg my dad to let me go there. My dad said it wasn't a Witches' Academy but a school. I didn't believe him. I thought he was lying because he didn't want me to be a witch when I grew up. Approximately thirty years later one of my children went to that very school; turns out my dad was right all along. And, I don't think he'd have minded if I'd become a witch, so long as my mischief was always merry.